# A Stone Cold Murder

# A Stone Cold Murder

**Reluctantly Psychic Murder Mystery**

Kris Bock

A Stone Cold Murder

Tule Publishing First Printing, April 2025

The Tule Publishing, Inc.



First Publication by Tule Publishing 2025

Cover design by Lee Hyat Designs



ISBN: 978-1-966593-32-4

## Dedication

For Phil, my favorite person.

Life is better with you in it.

# Reader Letter

If this is your first time reading one of my books, welcome! You can learn more about my other books on my website, www.krisbock.com. If you found me through my Accidental Detective mystery series or my romance, romantic suspense, or romantic comedy, thank you for giving this series a try too. Either way, I hope you enjoyed meeting Petra and her friends, allies, enemies, and animals.

Bonneville is loosely based on Fort Sumner, New Mexico, but the fictional Bonneville is a little larger and I've placed it farther west. The Banditt Museum was inspired by the Billy the Kid Museum in Fort Sumner, though all characters and plot elements are entirely fictional. The real museum is definitely worth a stop if you're driving through New Mexico on U.S. Route 60. You won't find Petra's geology wing there, but you will find relics of the Old West and thousands of other artifacts, from kids' toys to a horse-drawn hearse! For the exhibits in Petra's geology wing, I browsed the New Mexico Bureau of Geology Mineral Museum in Socorro, another great stop.

I hope to see you again for book 2, *Death at Rock Bottom.*

# Chapter One

IT'S NO FUN sorting through the belongings of a dead man. I assume that's true for most people, except maybe antique dealers or historians. But I think it's worse for me.

That's not because I'm a narcissist. (As far as I know. I admit I've never been tested.) It's because of my psychometry. It might sound cool to pick up vibrations left behind on objects, giving me glimpses of the items' histories. But I didn't want to know more about the man who'd had my job before me. Everything so far suggested Reggie Heap was an ordinary man who had more chest pains and heart palpitations than he let on. I might have warned him to get that checked out, if he hadn't already died of a massive heart attack that killed him even before his car ran off a mountain road.

It was my office now, and I needed to scrub away all traces of the former occupant. Does that sound harsh? I've lived with this gift, or curse, for thirty years, and I had to control it or it would drive me insane. I mean that literally, and not in the *My head literally exploded* actually figurative sense. Think about it like this: It might sound cool to have telepathy, if you assume you could choose when and where to use it. But imagine if you *had* to hear every thought of every person nearby.

Yeah, you'd probably just stay home.

Otherwise you might, oh, see a vision of your dad kissing someone who is not your mom, and accidentally destroy your parents' marriage at age five, just as an example. Or have your junior high friends pressure you to psychically spy on the boys they like to see if their feelings are returned. How about having word of your ability spread around high school, so everyone either thinks you're a liar or is afraid to let you touch them or anything they've touched?

I had to work my way through eight years of part-time college doing landscaping, because waiting tables or working retail would bring me into too much contact with strangers' items, and the constant barrage of information is exhausting, even when the information is tedious and unimportant. Psychometry has done very little good in my life so far.

Not being independently wealthy, or even aloofly middle class, I couldn't just stay home. I was about as far from a *people person* as one could be, so I needed a job that paid well enough that I could live alone, just me and my pets (ten at the current count). Ideally, the job wouldn't bring me into contact with a lot of other people or their stuff. I hoped I had that job now, working in a small museum in a tiny town in a state with something like twenty people per square mile.

Being a museum curator gave me a nice excuse to wear

white cotton gloves, although it might seem strange to do so while clearing the desk of family photos and stray pens. Fortunately, no one was around to ask. I didn't like wearing gloves though. I didn't want any information from my touch, but I felt oddly clumsy, like trying to clean a dimly lit room while wearing dark glasses.

I'd boxed up all the personal items, so it seemed safe to take off the gloves. I glanced at the four tall filing cabinets, which had decades of records of purchases and donations. Sorting through them would give me a good idea of what the collection held as well as a chance to make sure everything was properly filed. That would take days though, and it could wait. I started rubbing the desk down with a cleaning wipe.

Someone appeared in the doorway and said, "Knock, knock."

"Hello." I straightened, keeping the wipe in my right hand. I try to keep my hands full when I meet new people to discourage handshaking, but it doesn't always work. I dislike shaking hands, but not because of the psychometry. It's because I've read the statistics on how many people don't wash their hands after using the restroom.

He strode in and thrust out his hand. "I'm Kit Carson." He looked about midthirties, with brown hair and a thick brown beard that hung halfway down his chest.

I dropped the wipe and offered my hand a bit warily. I was confident I wasn't meeting the nineteenth-century frontiersman, but did he know that?

His handshake was firm, and he wore no rings that might give me an unwanted jolt of insight. He had a nice smile and long-lashed brown eyes that seemed ready to laugh. "Kit Carson Banditt, that is."

"Oh. You must be Peyton's . . ." Son or grandson? The museum's founder and owner was well into his seventies, so it could go either way.

"Grandson. I give tours, work in the office, and cover the front counter sometimes. Welcome to the Banditt Museum."

He gave my hand another squeeze. He'd held it for a weirdly long time, and believe me, I know all about weird. As far as the psychometry, I don't get that much information from touching someone's skin. Maybe a sense of their mood, but no more than you could get from studying facial expressions. But sometimes handshaking brings me into contact with a ring, watch, or sleeve. Emotions and memories seem to cling to inanimate objects longer, for some reason. Then I might learn that the boss at my temp job had not been on an *important phone call* for the last hour but rather having video sex with his boyfriend.

Okay, maybe my dislike of shaking hands did have to do with the psychometry. I really don't care what other people do, but I don't want to know about it. Also, and I cannot emphasize this enough, please wash your hands.

I withdrew my hand and tried to make my smile politely impersonal. "Thank you. I'm looking forward to getting settled in."

"If you get lost, just holler and someone will come find you." He chuckled, but the museum was a maze. Peyton had escorted me to my office, but I gave it about a twenty percent chance that I could find my way back to the entrance without at least three wrong turns. "Dad said you're an expert on rocks, but you ought to learn about all the other stuff we have here too. I'd be happy to show you around."

My nerves pulsed. "Peyton said I'd only have to work with the rocks and minerals, not the other artifacts."

I studied geology because rocks are quiet. They tell stories, in the layers of sand and pebbles deposited by seasonal floods, the crystal size that identifies plutonic versus other volcanic rocks, the clamshells and crinoids that prove some mountains were once underwater. But they don't shout with grief or anger or fear, the way human artifacts can. I'd taken the curator job with the understanding that I'd only have to work in my wing.

Kit shrugged. "If that's what interests you. But you might get questions from visitors, so it's good to know what else is here and how to find it. I have to tell you, the mineral wing isn't that popular. Most people only plan to stop at the museum for an hour or two, so by the time they get all the way back here, they've already spent more time than they planned and they're anxious to hit the road."

That sounded fine to me, but if I wanted to keep this job, I probably shouldn't tell the owner's grandson that I'd be happy to be left alone in the least popular section. I doubted I'd had much competition for the position, since the job didn't pay well, and most people wouldn't want to move to a town of 2000 people in New Mexico. But rent was cheap, I didn't care about access to the cafés and clubs you'd find in big cities, and there weren't a lot of job openings for geologists with bachelor's degrees who didn't want to go into oil, gas, or mining or substitute teach high school science.

"I'll try to update the collection to make it more appealing," I said. "I can't promise it will be the first stop for passing tourists, but maybe we'll give them a reason to make a longer stop on the way back."

"I wish you well, but I imagine the outlaws and lawmen will always be most popular." He smiled with the smug satisfaction of someone with job security. "If you're not a fan now, you will be once you hear the stories. All true!"

"Well, maybe I'll pick up a book from the gift shop."

He gave a derisive huff. "No need. I know everything there is to know, and I'm happy to share. We could talk over lunch sometime." He winked. "I like to think I'm more entertaining than a book written by some scholar."

"I'm sure," I said neutrally.

I wasn't sure if Kit was flirting, trying to relieve his boredom, or just aggressively friendly. If he led tours, he probably had to be outgoing and cheerful with strangers. The museum's survival depended on tourists, so they'd want to give people a great experience. Peyton had told me that most of the Banditt Museum's customers were people driving across country on Route 60. They looked for interesting places to stop for an hour or so in order to break up the drive, and the museum had good reviews. Visitors came for the stories and artifacts relating to the Wild West and, according to Peyton, often stayed for hours to explore all the little treasures in the sprawling, mazelike building and still left wishing they'd allowed more time for the visit.

I hoped Kit was this friendly with everyone. I had zero interest in dating, especially a coworker. It's too awkward with the psychometry. I don't want to tell someone I just met about it, because they'll think I'm crazy or lying. Or if they believe me, they back off because my ability is creepy. But if I wait until we get closer to tell them, it's like I'm invading their privacy up to that point. People don't like thinking you know things about them they haven't told you.

I glanced around the tiny office. "Well, I have lots to do here. Thanks for stopping by."

"Sure thing." He left with a cheerful wave.

I relaxed a little. He didn't seem offended by the brush-off, and he could take a hint. Or else he hadn't noticed the hint and would be persistently pesty.

I looked around the office. Besides the desk and file cabinets, it had wooden shelves along one wall. They held some rather nice geologic samples, though presumably not quite nice enough to make the main collection. I picked up a piece of smoky quartz. A prism, longer than my hand, thrust up like an obelisk from a cluster of smaller crystals at the base. A little label on the bottom confirmed my identification, while a clean spot on the shelf showed how much dust had piled up around the samples.

I might as well clean the shelf and its displays. While I was at it, I could check all the labels so if anyone asked about the specimens, I'd sound like I knew what I was talking about. The easiest way to clean rocks is to run them under gently flowing water, as long as they're not made up of minerals that dissolve easily. The museum might have an outside hose. It would take a few trips, but I could carry several specimens in a box at once.

Peyton had given me boxes for packing up Reggie Heap's stuff. I grabbed an empty one and started loading rocks and minerals into it. I'd definitely keep the frothy, seafoam-green Smithsonite. Maybe not the stringy bit of copper, which was interesting but not all that pretty.

A sample as big as two fists together was made up of cubic crystals in a lovely shade of lilac. Some marks showed where small pieces had broken off, which might be why it was in the office instead of on display. Fluorite, with some impurities to give it the purple shade? Tests could confirm that, but I wouldn't need them if it was properly labeled.

I picked it up with both hands.

*Rage. The desire to hurt.*

*Fear. An explosion of pain. Panic dissolving into darkness.*

I staggered and dropped the mineral. When my vision

cleared, I was leaning against the desk with both hands pressing down on it. Fortunately, I'd dropped the crystal cluster on the desk and not my foot. It would have been hard to explain breaking my foot in that manner.

But not as difficult as explaining why I thought these crystals had been used as a weapon.

# Chapter Two

I LEANED ON the desk and concentrated on breathing.

What was I going to do? I'd gotten overwhelming emotions from the mineral—I was going to call it fluorite until shown otherwise—but the images were jumbled. I had a very strong impression that someone had used the fluorite to hit someone else, but I couldn't identify the attacker or the victim. Nor could I see the outcome: injury, death, merely a headache?

Energy residue fades over time, and that had been like a punch to the brain, so whatever happened must've happened fairly recently—in the last few weeks, if not days. I closed my eyes and tried to recreate the images without actually touching the crystals again. Had I seen a corner of the desk? And some mottled brown carpet . . . like the carpet in this office.

"Are you all right?"

I gasped and jumped.

"Sorry! I didn't mean to startle you." Two women stood in the open doorway, the older one speaking. "You must be Petra. I'm Liberty and this is Haven. We stopped by to introduce ourselves, but you don't look well."

I tried to shove the emotions out of my mind and gather my wits. *Act normal. You can pretend to be normal.* "I just got lightheaded for a moment. I've been cleaning and probably kicked up some dust."

Liberty wrinkled her nose. "I can imagine. It builds up so quickly. Must have something to do with that desert all around us." She was probably in her early forties, with a lean, athletic build and a French braid the color of pale honey. She wore a white button-up shirt and longish denim shorts.

The other woman looked to be a few years younger than I was, early to mid-twenties. She had tawny skin, dark hair curling to her shoulders, and eyes so dark they might have been black. Her shirt had a design of retro Western travel postcards against a map background, and her orange lipstick matched one of the colors. She also wore shorts. Apparently the dress code was casual, perhaps in response to the warm weather that felt like spring although it was late February. She was studying me with equal curiosity.

"I'm sorry, I missed your name," I said.

She grinned. "It's Haven, Haven Gillooly. I curate the more modern stuff, anything from the nineteenth to twenty-first centuries, with a focus on the Wild West and Route 66 eras. Liberty handles historical eras prior to that—prehistoric, indigenous people, Spanish settlers. Also aliens."

I shifted my gaze to Liberty. Her shoulders twitched in a tiny shrug. "That's my hobby. And you can't have a museum of weird New Mexico without including the myths around

Roswell. Have you seen the dioramas? The aliens are one of our most popular photo ops."

"Um, no." I was getting way too much info at once, including the fact that everyone working at this museum seemed to have an odd name. Was that a prerequisite for working there? My name wasn't common in the US, but I didn't think it was particularly odd.

I dragged my thoughts back to the conversation, trying to ignore the fluorite sample that still throbbed at the edge of my awareness. "I've never been in the museum before today. We did the interview over video chat. I studied the website, of course."

"Right, you came from the northwest," Liberty said. "I know Peyton wanted to hire someone quickly after Reggie passed." She looked around the office, her gaze lingering on the boxes filled with Reggie's stuff, and then on the fluorite cluster that, I now noticed, had scratched the wooden desk. "I hope you're not uncomfortable taking over his office."

"Er, no." It wasn't like his ghost haunted the room. Not that I necessarily believed in ghosts, never having seen one myself, but I keep an open mind. But Reggie hadn't even died in the office.

Or had he? I'd been told he'd had a heart attack and his car ran off a winding mountain road. What if that wasn't true? Something had happened in that office, something violent, fairly recently. And the man who'd used this office was dead, violently, in a way that would cover up any injuries he might have had prior to the car accident. What if someone had killed him there in his office, with a mineral sample from his shelves, and then staged the car accident to cover up the crime?

My vision went gray around the edges. I propped a hip on the edge of the desk, but not close enough to risk brushing against the crystals, and focused on breathing.

"I'm giving the office a thorough cleaning and doing some redecorating," I said. "I admit it is strange taking over an office when the previous person didn't have a chance to clear out his stuff." I hesitated and then plunged forward. "What was Reggie like?"

*Was he the kind of person someone would want to kill?*

Obviously I couldn't ask that. Maybe I could find out something though. Ideally something that would prove I was wrong about the feelings I'd sensed. Maybe they'd used the crystals in amateur theatrics. The people involved would have to be really good actors to get that much emotion imprinted into the fluorite. I still felt queasy in reaction to the violence. But if they'd performed a scene over and over, that could explain why the emotional residue was so strong. Maybe. I'd never actually tested theatrical props, but I might be able to convince myself it would work that way. Why anyone would be practicing in this office was another question. Could other businesses around town have the same carpet? It didn't seem likely, but maybe if a supplier got a great deal on the ugly stuff . . . I was grasping at straws.

Slippery, insubstantial ones.

Liberty and Haven exchanged glances. Did the silence last too long? Or were they merely giving each other the chance to answer first?

"He was an odd duck," Liberty said at last. "I know you're not supposed to speak ill of the dead, but frankly, if you meet anyone in this town who isn't odd, they probably won't last long." One corner of her mouth twitched up. "Present company not excepted. I've been here over ten years. Reggie was only here for, what, two or three years?"

"He came right before I did," Haven said. "I've been here almost two years."

"I gather he'd bounced around a lot," Liberty said. "He was in his fifties—fairly young to die of a heart attack, but a bit old to start over at a museum like this. People usually work here at the start of their careers, when they can't find anything better"—she nodded at Haven—"or when they run out of options. We're tolerant of quirks."

That was good for me. I wondered what it said about Liberty.

"It's a fun place to work though." Haven bounced slightly, like she was bopping to music only she could hear. "I'm sure you'll enjoy it!"

"I'm sure I will. So Reggie didn't have a family?"

"Not that he ever mentioned," Liberty said. "He lived alone here. I don't know if he had a spouse in the past, or children somewhere." She was studying me curiously. Did my questions seem peculiar? I wasn't sure I could even tell anymore.

"I have a couple of boxes of his stuff," I said by way of explanation. "I don't know who should get it."

"Ah. Take it to the office and let the Banditts deal with it," Liberty said.

"Thanks, I'll do that." I should probably change the subject before they got suspicious, but I couldn't stop thinking about Reggie. "You don't think any of his friends will want a memento?"

"I wouldn't say he had any close friends," Liberty said. "He kept to himself."

"That's a little sad." I wasn't one to speak, since I did the same, but I was growing more determined to understand what had happened with the crystals, and to do that I might need to understand the man who'd had this office before me. "No family, no friends, and either no career ambitions or he'd failed to achieve them. Not much of a eulogy."

Liberty nodded. "I guess there's a lesson there. Live as you want to be remembered? I really can't say much about Reggie except he was harmless."

"He is now anyway." Haven slapped a hand over her mouth to muffle a giggle. "Sorry. Inappropriate."

"I told you we're all a little weird around here," Liberty said.

"Honestly, that doesn't even register on my weirdness scale." That was, in fact, the truest thing I'd said yet.

"Well, you'll fit right in." Liberty cocked her head. "You never met Reggie?"

"I'd never heard of him until I applied for this job, and he was already dead. Why?"

She shook her head. I raised my eyebrows. It seemed like a strange question, and anything unusual interested me at the moment. Of course, the problem with moving to a new town, starting a new job, and meeting new people is that pretty much everything is out of the ordinary.

She shrugged. "You're in the same field. You might have crossed paths before."

"I suppose, but geology isn't that small a field." Maybe you'd meet people around the country if you got to the PhD level and went to a lot of conferences, but I was a nobody. It sounded like Reggie was the same.

Haven had been watching us, her gaze shifting back and forth as if watching a tennis match. Did she seem unnaturally tense? Or was I so thrown out of step by what I'd gotten from the fluorite that everything seemed odd and wrong?

Liberty glanced over her shoulder, where distant voices murmured, presumably visitors to the museum. "I guess we should get to work. You're welcome to join us for lunch."

Haven nodded. "We take lunch at one, Liberty and me, unless there's a big tour group scheduled or it's especially crowded and they need us to help with tours or the front counter."

Great. It sounded like everyone was expected to pitch in

wherever needed, which made sense for such a small operation, but why had Peyton told me I'd only have to handle the rocks and minerals wing? Had he said that to get me out here, assuming once I'd moved he could change the rules and I'd be forced to give in? Now if I insisted on following our agreement, I'd look like a jerk and not a team player.

Maybe I could compromise and agree to give tours—which was terrifying in its own way, because I didn't have a lot of experience dealing with strangers or being friendly, but I wouldn't have to actually touch any of the artifacts in the museum. Then I'd insist on not working the counter where I'd have to take people's money and credit cards. Cash didn't usually carry strong impressions, since it changed hands too often, but *usually* wasn't *never*. And credit cards could pick up the energy of the person who carried them, sometimes with anxiety over how they were going to pay for the charges they were running up.

"But that's rare." Liberty was studying my face. It's possible I hadn't kept my expression as blank as I'd intended. "Typically we have at most a couple dozen people in the museum at any given time, and Kit can handle the tours."

I swallowed and nodded.

"Kit takes lunch at noon," Haven said. "Reggie usually ate alone in this office. It's nice to have another woman here. Girl power!" She grinned, sunny and enthusiastic. She made me feel like a dragon who only wanted to crawl into its dark cave and hide away with its treasures, at least one of which was covered in blood. "So, lunch?"

For a moment, I was tempted. I could put aside my violent thoughts—or rather, my thoughts on what violence might have been done here. Walk away from the puzzle of the crystals. Forget about blood and pain.

And female friendship? Of course I wanted that. But I couldn't let people get too close. It was unfair to them if I kept my abilities secret, and dangerous to me if I revealed them.

"Thanks for the invite, but I need to make sure my animals are settling in at my house." I hadn't realized I'd need an excuse for avoiding socialization this soon, but I was glad I had one.

"Oh!" Haven bounced like an excited toddler. "What kind of animals?"

"Mostly small critters." I didn't want to run down the list and find out that such and such was her favorite, and could she come meet them? "It was quite the trip across the country. Twenty-four hours of driving over two and half days. I still have to wait for most of my stuff to arrive and then unpack it. It will probably be weeks before I get everything sorted."

"I'll bet," Liberty said, looking over her shoulder. "Well, see you around." She headed down the hall.

Haven smiled again. "Bye! Welcome to the Banditt Museum." She followed Liberty.

Well. On the bright side, it seemed other people working

at the museum were just as odd and awkward as I was, so I'd fit right in.

On the extremely gloomy side, I had a mineral sample telling me it had been used to hurt, maybe even kill, someone. What was I supposed to do about that? I imagined taking my claim to the police. I could almost hear their laughter. In a town this size, anyone I told might spread the word, and I'd be an outcast before I got my first paycheck. They might tolerate quirks, but I didn't want to out myself as a complete freak.

Whenever someone finds out about psychometry, the first question is, *Are you kidding me?* Well, actually the first question is usually, *What's that?* Once I explain, it's *You're kidding, right?* or some variation. The third question is along the lines of *Are you completely bonkers?* but that's more of an expression of disbelief than an actual question.

Anyway, once they start to believe in it—which usually only happens after extensive demonstrations—then the question is, *What do you know about me?* That one comes with a jolt of panic. Yeah, I don't even need to touch you to know you don't want me reading your mind—it's there in your eyes. Because we all have secrets. Mostly not big secrets. Petty stuff like bad habits or pleasures we've been told are shameful. Biting one's nails, or preferring the remake to the original song.

That's why I haven't told anyone in fifteen years. It's easier if people don't know. But then I feel guilty keeping secrets from them, especially secrets about how easily I could learn their secrets. So it's simpler to not make friends at all.

I generally try my hardest *not* to learn people's secrets, both out of respect for their privacy and because I don't want to know that much about other people. But the fluorite wasn't merely whispering something that might be embarrassing gossip. It was screaming violence.

Could I simply ignore it? Convince myself I'd been mistaken, or it hadn't been as bad as I'd thought?

Maybe I was picking up vibrations from a crime that had already been solved, the attacker caught and the case closed. But wouldn't the police have confiscated the mineral sample if they'd known it had been used in a crime? If they'd eventually given it back, would Reggie have left something used as a weapon on his shelf like that? It was a nice sample, but not so spectacular that you'd treasure it despite its bloody history, like the Hope Diamond.

Come to think of it, the museum had displays of guns supposedly used by Old West outlaws and sheriffs to kill each other. If someone had used the fluorite to commit murder, it probably wouldn't be hidden away in a curator's office. It would be on display as another morbid tourist attraction.

So if the fluorite had been used as a weapon, I was likely the only person who knew about it—other than the attacker, that is.

I didn't see anything I could definitely identify as blood

on the crystals, though something dark had seeped into some of the fissures. I could try to find a magnifying glass and take a closer look. But then what? I didn't know how to prove it was blood. I didn't know how to tell whose blood it was. And I still couldn't go to the police. Any regular person would assume a few smears of blood had probably come from some minor accident, perhaps far in the past.

Maybe I was wrong. I could pretend I believed that. I could wrap the fluorite in a towel before I picked it up and hide it away somewhere, or throw it out, or at least shift it to a display where I wouldn't have to see it every moment I was in the office. Anyone else who had taken this job would have treated the fluorite like a pretty mineral sample, nothing more. Why should I be different?

It eventually came down to a simple question. Could I live with myself if I did nothing?

Darn it. I hate it when I have ethics.

I had to do something. At least try to learn more about what had happened. If I could capture a bit more of the vision, maybe I'd see the victim. Then I could find out whether they were alive and uninjured—or not.

I closed my office door. The door was basically a glass panel inside a frame, so closing it wouldn't keep anyone from seeing me in the office and expecting me to answer if they knocked. Still, it would give me an extra second or two of notice—and maybe discourage people from wandering in to say *hi*, being all friendly and welcoming, the jerks.

I sat at the desk and drank a few swallows of the now-tepid tea I'd brought in with me. When I leaned forward to look through the door glass, nobody seemed to be around. It might be better to wait until after hours, or to take the crystal cluster home with me, but I wouldn't be able to concentrate on anything else until I dealt with this.

I took three deep breaths, and then two more, before admitting I was delaying. I reached for the fluorite.

My hands settled on the mineral, fingers sliding into gaps between the large crystals. I'd braced myself, but the vision still flooded me, nasty and sharp like downing a shot of cheap tequila. A jumble of anger, pain, shock—*What have I done?*

# Chapter Three

I GASPED FOR air as my arms thrummed with tension. "Let . . . go," I commanded my hands. I had to peel my fingers off one at a time. I ached from my fingertips to my neck, as if I'd been holding the fluorite out in front of me for an hour and then, for a little extra fun, it had zapped me with an electric shock.

I sank back into my chair, trying to make sense of the images and feelings. I was more convinced than ever that the fluorite had been used as a weapon, and probably a fatal one. The vision, if you could even call it that when I'd seen so little, was like looking through a turning kaleidoscope. I was pretty sure the scene had been this office—same carpet, a corner of the same desk. There might be other rooms in the museum with the same décor though. The museum wasn't all carpeted, but they might have used the same carpet in other offices, bought the same desks.

But the fluorite fit on that shelf, it made sense in this department, not anywhere else. I had no straws left to grasp. It had happened here.

I'd also glimpsed what I interpreted as legs in blue jeans

stretched out on the floor. That had quickly been followed by the feeling, as strong as a shout, of *What have I done?*

I tried to pick apart that feeling. The attacker had been shocked at his audacity but also oddly elated. His success made him feel powerful.

Ick. Is it any wonder I don't want to know more about people than I absolutely must?

But I had to keep analyzing. Without thinking about it, I'd identified the attacker as male—*his* audacity, *his* success. But was I assuming that the person yielding the weapon was a man because men were, on average, more violent than women, or was I actually getting a masculine vibe from the tangled feelings?

I wasn't sure. In my experience, psychometry could pick up what I thought of as female or male energy—but that didn't necessarily identify the person's sex. Some men had more female energy and some women had more male energy. (And I really wished I had better terms for it, because gender is a construct and all, but I didn't. Gender is a construct by a society that still teaches us to think of aggression and confidence as male, while nurturing is female, and I grew up in this society.)

I rolled my stiff shoulders and shook out my hands to ease the stinging feeling. I still had to figure out what to do with the stupid fluorite. I didn't want to touch it again. And now it had my fingerprints on it. Right, I should've thought of that earlier. The smooth planes of the crystals probably took fingerprints well.

I wasn't worried about getting blamed for the crime. I had a legitimate reason for my fingerprints to be there, and a good alibi for whatever had happened, because it was almost certainly before I'd entered New Mexico the day before. But I might have destroyed any prior fingerprints. Though surely if someone had used it as a weapon, he—they—would have cleaned the fluorite afterward, though close examination with a magnifying lens, or even fancier technology in a CSI lab might turn up traces of blood. But, as noted, that did me little good.

I tipped my head back and closed my eyes. This was not how I'd hoped my first day would go. I had more than enough to do without dealing with stupid killers and their stupid weapons.

A rap at the door jolted me out of my thoughts. What disaster awaited me now?

Peyton Banditt opened the door without waiting for my response. This particular potential disaster was my new boss, who had possibly lured me to the middle of nowhere with job promises he didn't intend to keep. He was a barrel-chested man, maybe around five foot six, with a thick white beard. His mustaches swooped down before curling up again, framing his mouth with a pair of tildes. His white eyebrows swooped too.

He beamed paternally. "Petra, my dear. How are you settling in?"

*I'm completely unsettled.*

"I'm getting there. I've been cleaning the office."

He looked at the fluorite cluster on my desk. "Choosing a few favorites to keep back here?" He grabbed it with both hands and lifted it.

I tensed, partly because to me, touching that mineral sample was painful, and partly because it now had an additional set of finger and palm prints all over it. Good thing I hadn't been planning to take the fluorite to the police.

I cleared my throat. "That was on the shelf back here. Do you know if it was part of your collection or if Mr. Heap brought it in?"

Peyton turned it over. "This looks like our numbering system. It should be in the files if you want to know more about it."

"Oh, good. I'm not sure what to do with stuff that belonged to my predecessor. Should I box it up for his heirs?"

Peyton set the fluorite on a clean stretch of shelf and glanced around the office. "I'm not aware that Reggie had any close family members. If you find something valuable, let me know, but otherwise feel free to toss things or keep anything of use to you."

That hurt. I'd never even met Reggie, but it felt tragic that the people he'd seen every day didn't seem to be mourning him. The crystal that might have been used to kill him would remember him longer.

Peyton peered at me. "Are you quite all right?"

I like to think I keep my feelings hidden, but I may be wrong. "Fine. Just tired and a bit overwhelmed by the move. There's a lot to do."

He nodded. "As I said in our interview, I'm excited to get that big new donation organized and items put on display. And while I hate to speak ill of the dead, I suspect poor Reggie wasn't up to the task." He glanced around as if someone might be listening in this empty, unpopular wing of the museum—maybe Reggie's ghost. "He made very few changes the entire time he was here. The storeroom is cluttered and disorganized . . . But I don't mean to distress you more. Possibly you'll find Reggie did a lot of work on the files." He looked doubtful.

"Er, would you like to have a seat?"

I was sitting behind my desk while my boss, a man two and a half times my age, stood. It felt weird inviting him to sit in a room he actually owned, when the guest chair was right in front of him, but maybe he was old-fashioned. He wasn't *that* old, but running a museum like this might keep people locked in the past.

He flicked his fingers, brushing away the suggestion. "Sitting too much isn't good for you. My doctor says I have the heart of a much younger man, no doubt because the museum keeps me active in body and mind."

I couldn't think of anything to say. I could think of many things I *wanted* to say—What happened in this office?

Why is everyone so friendly to me but indifferent about a man who died? Did Reggie Heap really die of a heart attack, or was he hit by a very pretty cluster of fluorite crystals? Is this museum a hotbed of . . . I don't even know what.

Did you lure me here to be the next victim?

But I couldn't say any of that. Best case scenario, Peyton Banditt wouldn't know the answers, and I'd sound like I was having a psychotic break. If he could answer those questions, then he was dangerous, and I didn't want him to know I suspected anything.

"In any case, I just stopped by to make sure you didn't need anything, and to see if you'd care to join Mrs. Banditt and myself for lunch. My treat." He beamed.

What was this obsession everyone had with lunch? Did I look malnourished? Was working in the museum so dull that the staff scheduled their days around their lunch break?

"Thank you, that's very kind."

It was harder turning down my boss's invitation than one that came from coworkers. But I had to, since I'd already told Liberty and Haven I had plans, and I really did need to check on my animals. Plus, I desperately needed a break from people, especially these friendly strangers poking at my walls. If I didn't shore up those barricades, someone might find a gap to break through. I needed to surround myself with purring cats and squeaking guinea pigs and calm the heck down so I could figure out what to do.

"Perhaps another time though?" I suggested. "I have pets

who are probably also feeling overwhelmed by the move. I ought to check on them."

He nodded. "Of course. Later this week then. I trust the house is satisfactory?"

"It's great." Finally I could say something honestly and with warmth. "Thank you for connecting me with the owner."

"Oh, I was delighted to do you both a favor. Shelley's an old friend."

It truly was a great house, old and rather shabby but big, with three bedrooms and a yard. And I was paying less in rent than I had for my tiny apartment near Seattle. I hadn't thought to question why it was available. Rent might be cheap here, but there probably wasn't a lot of turnover. Was I living in Reggie Heap's old place? I didn't want to ask, in case my interest in Reggie started to seem suspicious.

Peyton paced the tiny room, his gaze flickering over the half-empty shelves, the box of mineral samples, the filing cabinets stuffed so full drawers couldn't close. He touched the fluorite crystals again, shifting the sample slightly on the shelf. Was his attention to it suspicious? Or did he simply like things tidy, and the purple crystals were bright enough to catch his attention?

"Forget what I said about the new collection. I'm not expecting you to get everything under control this week." He beamed a Santa Claus smile. "Someone young and energetic! That's just what this position needs."

My hands and arms ached. Anxiety filled my head, jumbling my thoughts so I couldn't get words out. Who said young people had all the energy?

"What do you intend to do with those?" He gestured toward the box of smaller rocks and minerals I'd pulled from the shelves.

"Clean them, for starters. Is there a hose somewhere I can use to get the dust off?"

"Oh, you haven't seen the workroom yet! Come with me."

I scrambled to follow him out of the office. He turned left and went through a door I hadn't noticed yet. To get to the big room that was now my domain, I'd walked through a dozen other rooms and narrow passages. Even the latter were lined with glass cases full of less valuable artifacts—someone's donated BB gun collection, Barbies through the ages, reproduction WANTED posters of the Wild West. It seemed the Banditt Museum had never met a donation it didn't deem worthy of putting on display.

It turned out this door, maybe fifteen feet from my office, led directly outside. Peyton nudged a rock with his foot to block the door open.

I stepped out behind the museum. The building surrounded three sides of the yard, but not in a nice U shape. Rather, pieces of building jutted out seemingly at random. Clearly the museum had once been much smaller, and rooms had been added on as needed, without a master plan—unless the master plan was *Build something that looks like it was constructed by drunken gremlins working in the dark from upside down blueprints.* A chain-link fence closed off the fourth side of the yard, with hardpacked dirt on our side and weeds and bushes beyond.

The yard itself was cluttered with old farming and mining equipment, plus a couple of vehicles that must not have been interesting enough to make it into the exhibit room filled with classic cars and horse-drawn wagons. It was still nice to be outside, away from the office that had turned claustrophobic with the echoes of violence. I breathed deeply of the warm, dry air and tipped my face to catch the sun.

I groped for something to say. "Can I use this door as a shortcut to my office?"

"You can come out this way, but it locks automatically, so you'll have to prop it open to return that way. Obviously I'd prefer you only do that if you stay close. I believe Reggie stepped out to smoke sometimes."

"I don't smoke."

"Very wise."

He strode to the next piece of jutting building, unlocked a door, and flicked on the lights as we stepped inside. We were in a room about twenty feet by forty feet, with no other doors or windows, unless they were hidden behind the floor-to-ceiling metal shelves filled with boxes and unidentifiable objects. A long row of metal tables ran down the center of the room, and a big utility sink sat near the door.

"This is where we store donations until someone has time to sort them and decide what goes on display," Peyton said. "If we get donations that aren't suitable for the museum, we sell them. We have a few people on call who specialize in particular artifacts—old license plates, neon signs, and so forth—and twice a year we have a big antique sale."

He started down the room. "Our recent geological donation is here in the back."

A section of shelves was crammed with cardboard boxes with the word GEO scribbled in black ink. Some boxes were collapsing under the weight of the ones on top of them. Good thing most rocks and minerals are fairly sturdy. If those boxes contained any delicate samples, I hoped they'd been packed with padding.

"I expect you'll spend most of your time back here for a while," Peyton said. "It might take a couple of months to sort all this."

Good, that was almost realistic. During our interview, he'd mentioned a big recent donation that needed to be sorted. I hadn't imagined this.

"You can clean things at the sink and decide what should go on display," he said. "Choose what to pull from the current collection to make room. Set aside anything to be sold. Perhaps you know a good way to sell rocks?"

I nodded. "It'll probably be worth setting up a table at some rock and mineral shows to start. If we price things reasonably, we can reduce inventory a lot over a weekend. Then how about having small samples for sale in the museum? A lot of kids love pretty rocks."

"See!" Peyton beamed and patted my back. "That's the kind of creative thinking we need here."

Other mineral museums did that, but if he wanted to think I was brilliant . . .

"Consider this room your domain for the foreseeable future. Let's see, it's almost March, so you'll have about two months before it's too hot to work out here."

Expect overwhelming heat by May. Good to know.

Peyton strode back down the room. "I think Reggie got started." He stopped where a box sat on the table with a few mineral samples next to it and more inside. "Looks like he didn't get very far. Poor fellow." Peyton heaved a sigh. "Well, he's in a better place now, I hope."

He hoped? Was that doubt about an afterlife, or concern over which direction Reggie might have gone?

I scanned the items, mainly small mineral samples. Some geodes that had been cut and polished. Several pieces of iron pyrite, or fool's gold, but none that the average person would mistake for real gold. A few minerals I didn't recognize, but really nothing notable. Still, I found myself reluctant to touch anything. How odd that Reggie had literally walked away in the middle of sorting this box and never returned. Was it merely a coincidence that he had died—perhaps violently—right after starting to sort this new donation?

A donation that was now mine to handle. I shivered despite the warm, stuffy room. What if Reggie Heap had been killed over something in this donation? I was definitely jumping from random guess to wild conclusion, but my thoughts kept racing ahead, driven by panic that logic couldn't control. If that *what if* was true, then maybe whoever had killed him had taken whatever they wanted, and they wouldn't be back. Finally, a comforting idea.

But maybe not. Maybe they hadn't found what they wanted yet. Maybe Reggie had been involved in something else, no idea what, that had gotten him attacked. Or maybe I was on the wrong track entirely. I was getting lightheaded again. When Peyton led the way back outside, I stumbled after him gratefully.

He closed the workshop. "It doesn't always latch properly, so be sure to check. I'll have someone bring you that key this afternoon."

"Okay, thanks." I looked up at the vivid blue New Mexico sky. It helped ease the claustrophobia of the storeroom, with the looming weight of all those artifacts ready to whisper their secrets. "I guess I'll be busy for a while."

"When I started this museum, people thought I was crazy. For the first few months, when no one came, I wondered if they were right. But I kept building my collection. I helped people clear out their attics and hauled away what they saw as junk."

That sounded like my nightmares.

He went on. "If someone had old mining equipment in their yard, I asked if I could take it. We advertised, put up a billboard along the highway—back in those days, no internet, no TripAdvisor or Yelp! And we grew, until I could quit my job, and then my wife could quit hers, and we could run the museum full-time."

I nodded. He'd basically told me the same thing during our interview. He was clearly proud of building the museum, and I guess anyone who follows a dream and succeeds should be proud.

"Now I want to leave a legacy," he said. "I thought my children would take over, but my son passed away, and the girls moved and married, and Kit . . . Kit isn't ready. Well. At least I have some life in me yet! So we are going to take this from a *quirky little roadside attraction*"—that sounded like he was quoting something, maybe one of those online reviews—"to a museum respected around the world."

He grabbed my shoulder and squeezed, his grip strong enough that I buckled under it. "And you're going to help me. Reggie was a mistake." He let go and turned away, gazing out at the collection of trash—or treasure—littering the yard. "Poor fellow," he added, almost as an afterthought.

He turned back toward me. With the sun behind him, his face was in shadow, his white hair lit like a halo. "I hope you'll fit in here. You don't strike me as the type to quit and have kids at the first opportunity. This is a good place to live, if you can handle it. Ask Liberty. She's been here over ten years. She pulled together a great Paleolithic display. Maybe a bit too academic though, with all the information about identifying arrowheads and spear points. People don't want to do that much reading in a museum."

"Right." Some kind of reply seemed necessary, although maybe he would keep talking regardless of my response, or my presence.

I was still trying to process that bit about having kids. I didn't plan or expect to have children, given the challenges I had dating or living with other people, but Peyton couldn't know that. What had he seen that told him I wasn't cut out to be a mother? I'm fairly average looking, I think. A bit androgynous with my short hair and lack of curves. Maybe he assumed I was gay. If so, it didn't seem to bother him, which was a relief. One of my concerns about moving to such a small town was the fear that people would be less tolerant than I was used to.

"I want our geology wing to be listed among the top mineral museums in the state," he said.

How many great mineral museums could a sparsely populated state like New Mexico have? I didn't ask, but I made a mental note to do a search later. Maybe I could tour them and call it part of my job. That could be fun. And get me away from this place, if only for a few days.

"I didn't want a PhD for this position," he said.

Good thing, because he wasn't paying enough for one.

He paced, gesturing with his hands. "We want to appeal

to the general public, lots of color and flash, but everything accurate too. Nothing that would let an academic scoff at the collection. Plenty to educate school groups."

"I'll do my best."

"I know you will." He beamed at me, an oddly proud look, more *grandfather* than *new boss*. It gave me a funny, twisty feeling inside. I didn't want to suspect him of anything. I wanted to believe I'd found a lovely little place that could become my home, with interesting work and coworkers I respected and enjoyed, even if I had to hold them at arm's length when they treated me like a friend.

"Now you get along home to your animals," he said. "We'll have time enough for everything else. There's a gate in that corner." He pointed. "It has a combination lock, 1859, the year Billy the Kid was born."

"Cool." I wasn't sure I'd remember Billy the Kid's birth year, but at least I could look it up if I forgot. For something to say, I added, "I'm looking forward to getting started."

Peyton beamed and patted my back again. "I think you'll fit right in here."

I wasn't sure that was a compliment, but he was probably right.

## Chapter Four

WE WENT BACK into the museum. Peyton said goodbye absently, frowning over whatever was in his thoughts, and left me. Buoyed by Peyton's enthusiasm, I was getting excited about updating the geology wing. It sounded like he wanted the museum to be everything to everyone, which was impossible, but that made things interesting. Average people, including children, could ooh and ah over pretty, colorful mineral samples such as the fluorite—no, not the fluorite, I wouldn't put that on display, but things like it. Add exhibits that taught science and history. Why different types of crystals grew in those particular ways. Pretty crystal formations *and* education. Something on the mining history of New Mexico, with equipment and local mineral samples. The geology wing had those items now, but they were all jumbled and random. Could I figure out something safe enough for a hands-on angle? If the collection had enough minerals that glowed under black light, I'd curtain off an area so people could see the samples in light, in darkness, and under black light. That was always a crowd pleaser.

I avoided looking at the fluorite as I grabbed my backpack. This job could be *fun*, if I could get past that horrible vision and all the questions surrounding it. Faint tremors seemed to ripple over my skin. I stretched out my hand to see if it was trembling, but any shivers must've been internal.

I'd worry about the fluorite and its message later. At the moment I felt queasy and headachy, exhausted from the long drive to New Mexico, anxious from trying to make a halfway decent impression on new people, and off-balance from the unexpected psychic vision. I needed to escape for an hour.

I locked my office door and scooted out the back. The gate in the fence had a chain with a padlock. Let's see, Billy the Kid's birth year. That would definitely start with eighteen. Then it was fifty-something? I tried a couple of numbers until I got it.

That wasn't great security, but an intruder could get through the chain with a bolt cutter anyway. The chain-link fence was about six feet high, with loops of razor wire on top. Get a ladder, throw a thick blanket over the top, and you could scale that easily enough. I glanced back at the building. I didn't spot any cameras, but that didn't mean there weren't any.

My commute now meant walking down the main drag for a couple of blocks and then turning onto the long street that led to my rental. It was such a small town. Two thousand people. My high school had that many students. I'd driven to work that morning, because that was how one got to work in my experience. Then I'd felt extremely foolish.

The museum was just over half a mile from my house. I'd walk home for lunch and leave my van at the museum so I could swing by the grocery store after work. I headed around the building to the main street.

The museum had a lot of antiques, but nothing small, portable, and extremely valuable, like rare gems or paintings by famous masters. The most valuable artifacts there would be hard to sell. You couldn't just offer Kit Carson's rifle on eBay without evidence that it had really belonged to him. The rusting farm equipment and dented cars in the yard weren't even important enough to put under shelter. The security was probably designed to keep bored teenagers from causing trouble.

It seemed unlikely an attack had happened during open hours, even in the quiet geology wing. The killer would have to hide the body right away, with the constant risk of somebody coming into the room. Had the person who wielded the crystal cluster as a weapon broken in after closing? Had they come into the museum as a visitor, paying their five dollars like the other tourists, and hidden until after hours?

Was it someone who worked in the museum?

I shivered despite the pleasant weather. How had I stumbled across violence here? Not that small towns were crime-free, but I'd expect drunk drivers and the occasional bar brawl. Maybe a rare murder due to a fight or domestic violence. As far as I could tell, the violence I'd sensed hadn't even been reported yet—but I should look at the news for the last few weeks. Did this town have a newspaper? They were dying off even in bigger cities. Maybe an online community bulletin board?

My landlady's house was right next door to mine, which might turn out convenient or annoying. She was trimming some bushes in her yard. "Hello! How was your first morning?" She stuck the hedge trimmers in a holster around her waist, wiped the back of her hand across her forehead, and grabbed her cane from where it leaned against the white picket fence around her yard.

I stopped across the fence from her. "Fine."

I'd fully exhausted my limited reservoir of sociability and desperately wanted to get inside under a pile of sweet fuzzballs, but I didn't want to start my residency by annoying the person who owned my rental. Plus she might know things about Reggie. Shelley was somewhere past seventy, with a limp that required her to use the cane. She seemed nice enough, and she had a Saint Bernard. Anyone who loves animals gains a few points with me. Toby got up from his spot in the shade and padded slowly toward me, long strands of drool dripping from his jowls.

"It's a little strange, cleaning up the office of someone who died." I gestured toward my place next door. "By the way, was that Reggie's house?"

She nodded. "I was glad to get another tenant in so soon. Peyton didn't waste any time in hiring you!"

"He seems anxious to get the geology wing updated and the new donation sorted."

"You'd think he could rest on his labors a bit, but that's not his style," she said fondly.

I needed to get more information without seeming like I wanted more information. "I'm trying to figure out what to do with the stuff Reggie left at the office. What did you do with his things?"

"I took his clothes and shoes to the thrift store. I washed the linens—they're in the closet at the end of the hall. He didn't have much else." She looked a little guilty. "His TV was nicer than mine, so I switched them."

"Makes sense. I wasn't expecting a furnished place anyway." I reached over the fence to rub Toby's head. "I suppose the furniture was Reggie's as well."

"Some of it has been in the house for years. If you need to get rid of things to make room for your own furniture, I'll put it in storage." She jerked her head toward the side yard. The shed behind the house must be her storage.

"Thanks. I'll let you know after my stuff arrives. They said two or three more days. I definitely won't need the bed, but maybe I'll keep the couch for the cats. It's a huge house for one person. It will be nice to have the space for my animals, and I'm very grateful you're willing to have so many pets there. It doesn't look like Reggie used a couple of the rooms at all."

"I don't know what that man did in his free time. He

was polite enough, with a hello when he passed by, unless he was wrapped in his own thoughts. But he didn't entertain much. No pets. I think he watched a lot of TV and played games on his computer. I saw the light sometimes, a glow from a screen."

"A loner," I said. "Well, I'm kind of that way too." I made a mental note to close the curtains or make sure my TV and laptop screens were facing away from the windows. That hadn't been a problem in my fourth-floor apartment. Not that any of my neighbors would have been interested in what I was doing anyway.

Shelley looked down at Toby. "What is it with these young people? They waste the best time of their lives." She looked back at me. "Well, it's probably good you don't want to party every night, although you can find some good two-stepping at the Rough Riders bar. And they have a mechanical bull!"

Toby expressed his opinion with a grumbling whine.

"I'm not much of a dancer. Or a bull rider." I hadn't meant to get talking about *me*. "Do you think that's why Reggie didn't go out much? He didn't find things to do around here?"

"Nah, I can't imagine him going out on the town even in a big city. You know the type, an awkward geek who was one step from living in his parents' basement. No criticism from me, as long as he paid his rent on time."

I smiled to show I'd gotten the hint. "I gather he did."

"Usually. Seems like the last few months, I had to go over and pound on his door to remind him of the date. He looked at me like I was talking in tongues, but then he'd shake himself out of it and write a check. Now I wonder if his heart problem was making him slow about things."

"Could be." Or the quiet loner had gotten caught up in something nasty and was distracted—and then dead.

"I had a pacemaker put in ten years ago." Shelley tapped her chest. "Felt like I had a whole new heart! They say you're slowing down because you're old, but don't believe them. You have to fight the doctors to make them treat you like a human being instead of someone with one foot in the graveyard."

I nodded, trying to look sympathetic, although aging wasn't the biggest problem in my immediate future. I was also realizing that Shelley put her own twist on idioms. Did she do it on purpose, as a joke? I couldn't ask, in case she didn't realize she was getting those sayings wrong.

I gave Toby a last pet. "Well, I'd better get moving if I want lunch and some time with my animals."

"Oh, is it lunchtime already? Thank goodness!" Shelley wiped her forehead again. "Come on, Toby, let's have some food and a nap. Take care, Petra." She limped toward her front door.

I went through the next gate. I had a yard! I could get dogs. I hadn't wanted to keep one in a small apartment. I thought living here would suit me very well—once I understood my weird vision with the fluorite crystals.

I unlocked the door. People probably didn't even lock up around here, but I wouldn't break that habit for a while, if ever. Certainly not if I suspected a killer was on the loose.

That was one more reason to find out what had really happened. It was hard enough to adjust to a new town, house, and job without worrying that someone I met was a murderer.

# Chapter Five

I STEPPED INTO the front room, the biggest room in the house. "I'm home!"

Jet, my black cat, raced down the hall toward me. He stopped about eight feet away, crouched, stared at me with pupils blown wide, and took off back down the hall. I'd named all my animals after minerals and gemstones, but Jet also fit his speed. Amber, my orange-and-white cat, was sprawled on the sofa. I petted her and she yawned and stretched. Onyx would be hiding.

I went into the room I'd allotted to the ferrets, since it had wood floors for easier cleanup. I could let them roam free in there unsupervised! Back home—or rather, in my prior apartment—they stayed in a cage while I was at work or school. Granted, they slept about twenty-three hours a day, and their cage had three levels with hammocks, blankets, toys, and litter boxes. Still, they liked lots of choices for sleeping, and they liked to explore or just check that everything was where it had been the day before.

I'd piled blankets on the bed and the floor and scattered the ferrets' toys. It took me a few minutes to track down all three of them. Tension eased out of me as we cuddled and played.

The next room held the two guinea pigs and two rats in their cages. Jet joined me there, sniffing at his buddies as I snuggled them. I didn't let the guinea pigs or rats out unsupervised. All my animals generally got along, but I couldn't risk the littler ones accidentally triggering the predator instinct from the cats or ferrets. Also, rats could get through remarkably tiny spaces and it was hard to track them down. I'd once lost Gypsum for a full day before she crawled out of the sleeve of my winter coat hanging in my closet. I still don't know how she got up to it.

After I'd seen everyone but Onyx, I wandered through the house. I'd had enough to manage taking myself and my animals across the country in my van. I'd had a moving container delivered to my building in Washington. I'd filled it, a truck had picked it up, and it would eventually make its way to me here. Maybe it didn't make financial sense to move my cheap stuff across country, but it only whispered secrets about me, and I already knew all of those. But since I was in Reggie's home, I could search the place for clues. At the same time, I could see if anything seemed safe to keep.

Furniture, some linens and towels (which I would not risk using) in the closet, dishes and the bare minimum of cookware in the kitchen, and small items such as soap dispensers and cleaning supplies. It was creepy knowing a man who might have been murdered had used these things.

What did they tell me about Reggie Heap? Was anything a clue to his death?

I wouldn't use my psychometry now, when I had to get through the afternoon at work. Psychometry could be draining, depending on what I was handling. Something made in a factory and shelved at a store likely hadn't spent enough time with any one person to carry emotion. A sweater worn occasionally might whisper of the wearer's last feelings, while a jacket worn every day for years got steeped in the owner's personality. But a powerful emotion lasting an hour could overwrite lesser emotions that built up for years. The intense emotions took the most out of me, whether a powerful one-time feeling or a buildup over a long time. Like they each stole a bit of my soul, one overly religious former friend had told me, but forget about her.

I'd never gotten a jolt like the one from the fluorite though. I hadn't known it was possible. It was kind of like knowing war exists and is terrible, versus joining the fighting. I needed to take an emotional step back if I was going to get through this. But later, I'd try searching the house with my extra sense—and hope I didn't freak myself out so much I couldn't bear to sleep there again.

My lunch hour was disappearing. I headed for the kitchen, Jet at my heels and sometimes in front of my ankles. I'd tried to use up everything I could before leaving Seattle. Most dry goods had been packed, so my cupboards were empty, but I had a jar of peanut butter from my road trip.

The refrigerator held food I'd brought with me: half a loaf of bread, some apples, and some hot sauces and marinades because I couldn't bear to throw them away and have to purchase them again. I definitely needed groceries. Good thing I had a credit card. Peyton had given me some money for moving expenses, with the agreement that I'd stay for at least a year, but that was long gone and my bank account was frighteningly low.

As I fixed my sandwich, I made a mental task list. It quickly got so long I moved it to my phone note app.

1. Get groceries, including cat food. (I used mail order for the other animals' special foods, and I had enough for a month.)
2. Clean the house, get rid of furniture I didn't want, and unpack.
3. Learn my way around town.
4. Find out a news source in town and see if anyone had been killed by a blow to the head, or if anyone was missing, in case Reggie wasn't the victim.
5. Learn more about Reggie Heap.
    a. Search for his name online.
    b. Search the house and his office for physical clues.
    c. Search the house and his office with psychometry for emotional clues.

That didn't even touch on the work I had to do at the

museum. I stopped before I got overwhelmed.

Jet stood at his bowl and mewed.

"You've had breakfast and it's too early for dinner."

He meowed again, clearly arguing. Amber trotted in, ever hopeful that one day Jet would convince me. I hardened my heart against their adorable faces. If I let them win once, I'd lose my status as alpha animal. Assuming I was the alpha; some days I had my doubts, and the animals probably did too.

The kitchen had a table and two chairs, but I ate my sandwich while standing. Moving was the worst. At least my old furniture should arrive soon. Sleeping on the floor was even less comfortable than sleeping in my van on the way here, but I refused to sleep in someone else's bed. Given what I was learning about Reggie, I was glad I hadn't risked it.

I washed stray peanut butter off my hands. Fortunately I'd kept a hand towel so I could wash my hands after packing. Unfortunately, I hadn't remembered to keep a bath towel for myself, so I'd had to borrow one of the old towels I'd packed in the ferrets' cage for my shower that morning. If I smelled a little like ferret musk, no one had mentioned it.

I grabbed an apple. Even with walking home, chatting with Shelley, and checking on my pack, I had ten minutes before I needed to head back to the museum. And that was assuming anyone cared or noticed how long I took for lunch. I'd play it safe until I got the rhythm of things.

Amber wound around my ankles, purring. Jet crouched by the food dishes and stared at me.

"Where's Onyx?" I asked.

No, I don't expect the cats to speak to me, either in words or telepathically. They're pretty good at letting me know when they want food (now, always). I knew the signs for *Pet me, love me, I'm your sweet little baby* and for *That's enough; I will bite if you touch me again.* They know how to communicate when they want to. But I don't get answers when I ask a question, such as, *Who dragged toilet paper all over the hallway, and how did you get the roll off the holder in the first place?* I'm sure they could answer, but they choose not to.

Amber put a paw on my knee and meowed. I scooped her up and held her in one arm, her head and front paws on my shoulder, while I resumed eating. She sniffed at the apple but didn't consider it food.

"I'm sure he's found a good hiding place," I said.

In my old apartment, Onyx had three or four favorite places to hide in case a stranger passed by in the hall, the doorbell rang, I accidentally made a loud noise, or a pigeon landed on the windowsill and freaked him out. He is not one of the feline world's tough guys. But I didn't know where he'd found to hide in this house. I'd searched the place well before releasing the animals and found no escape routes. Therefore, I was reasonably sure Onyx was still in the house somewhere, but I'd feel better if I found him.

"If you were Onyx, where would you hide?" I asked Jet.

He continued staring, probably trying to use mind control on me. He'd been rescued from the streets at about six months old. He was now five, but he hadn't given up on his dream of finding a memory-challenged human who would feed him a dozen times a day.

Amber crawled up on my shoulder.

"Ouch, watch the claws!"

She jumped to the top of the refrigerator. A hiss and a slight scuffling sound followed.

The top of the fridge was above my line of sight, so I stood on a chair. Onyx was hiding in the eight inches of space above the fridge and below a cabinet I would never use because it was too hard to reach. He was black with a white bib, which made him almost invisible in the shadowy space, but he stood out against fluffy, orange Amber next to him. It was probably my imagination that she looked smug as she started grooming Onyx's ear.

"Hi, baby," I said softly. "It's okay. You keep right on hiding if that makes you feel safe."

While I was up there, I might as well check the cabinet for anything a prior resident had left behind, like ancient to-go containers or instructions for long-gone appliances. When I'd explored the house, I'd peered around the fridge to make sure the cats couldn't get stuck back there or find a wormhole to another dimension, but I didn't actually check the cabinet.

I opened the door. Inside was a silver laptop computer.

Well, that was a surprise. Could it be Reggie's? It looked kind of chunky by today's standards, but it couldn't be too many decades old. Besides, surely no one would store a laptop up there and forget about it when they moved. But Shelley might have missed it when she cleared out Reggie's things.

If it was Reggie's, why was it in such an awkward place? Maybe he'd gotten a newer one and stuck the old one out of the way. Shelley had mentioned his computer, which I hadn't seen, but she might have claimed it for herself or donated it.

Or maybe this was his only computer, and he didn't want anyone else to find it. But he lived alone and didn't entertain, so who would see it? A thief looking for valuables? That seemed a bit paranoid—unless he *really* didn't want anyone to see what was on it.

What could be so secret?

I didn't want to touch the laptop. Something like that could have years of the user's emotions seeping into it. But it might hold a valuable clue. I used the hand towel to pick up the laptop, set it on the counter, and got down.

Jet had given up on trying to mind control me and was crunching on a stray piece of kibble on the floor. Wait a minute. He had been staring at me—and the top of the fridge, which would be behind me in his line of sight—when I'd asked about Onyx.

I narrowed my gaze at him. "You *can* understand me, can't you? You just choose to ignore my questions most of the time."

He ignored me, which seemed an appropriate answer.

I had gloves in my pocket, so I put them on before I opened the laptop and turned it on. A screen came up asking for a password. I was disappointed, but not surprised. Someone who hid his laptop wouldn't make it too easy to get into. It also showed a low battery. The power cord hadn't been in the cupboard, and I hadn't seen it in the house. I needed to charge the laptop before I spent time trying to figure out the password.

(I'm not a hacker, but maybe I wouldn't need to be. Geologists aren't necessarily known for keeping on top of technology, given that we're comfortable with the geologic timescale, where the *modern* era covers over 11,000 years. Maybe Reggie had used lousy passwords like *password* or his birthdate, regardless of how paranoid he might be. As I learned more about Reggie, I might get clues to words or numbers he could have used. And if all that failed, I could probably hire a fifteen-year-old on the internet to break into the laptop for me.)

I powered down the laptop, wrapped it in the towel, and put it in my backpack. Reggie might have left the power cord in his office.

I'd added even more items to my task list, but I'd also made progress. Surely Reggie's computer would tell me something about him! (*If it's really his*, a little voice whispered. *Hush*, little voice.) And if the computer worked, and Reggie didn't have heirs to claim it, maybe finders keepers applied. Shelley thought it had with the TV. I'd gone through eight years of part-time college doing assignments on my phone or at the campus computer lab. Getting a free laptop might be worth the hassle of dealing with something used. I could get a separate keyboard to plug into it, so I didn't have to touch the keys.

But enough fantasizing about my bright future. My lunch break was over.

"Thanks, guys," I told the cats. "See you tonight."

# Chapter Six

BACK AT REGGIE'S office—*my* office—I put on a pair of thin white cotton gloves I bought by the carton and started searching. Museum curators often use those gloves when handling items that would be damaged by the oils on one's skin, like photos and filmstrips. Most people probably didn't think rocks and minerals counted, but some minerals can be sensitive to oils, so much so that a fingerprint could become permanent.

Was that true with fluorite? Contrary to common belief, geologists don't instantly recognize every mineral and know all its properties. We might focus on volcanoes, earthquakes, geophysics, or engineering . . . the list goes on. With only a BS degree, I hadn't chosen a specialty yet, and I certainly didn't know the thousands of minerals with all their variations.

I'd looked up some of the common minerals in New Mexico, in case I got quizzed or people brought in samples for me to identify. I expected to see a lot of jasper and chalcedony, which are quartz variations, and some marine fossils since southern New Mexico used to be covered by a shallow sea. Also probably a lot of chert, which often breaks into small, triangular pieces that people want to believe are arrowheads. (Spoiler alert: They usually aren't.)

The geology wing was surprisingly quiet, at least in comparison to my morning full of visiting colleagues. A few groups of tourists came in, looked around briefly, and headed out again. A skinny man with black hair and tan skin spent half an hour loitering, shooting glances at me through the office door as I went through Reggie's desk. I had no idea what that was about and didn't want to ask. Eventually he left.

I didn't find anything suspicious in Reggie's desk. Of course, I didn't know what I was looking for, so it's entirely possible I missed whole catalogs of suspiciousness. I also didn't find a power cord for his laptop. That was odd. He wouldn't have a laptop without a power cord. But was it suspiciously odd, or randomly odd? I'd kept a sunglass case for a year because I was sure the sunglasses had to be in my apartment. I finally threw out the case while I was packing, which probably meant I'd find the sunglasses when I unpacked. Life can be so random that way you'd swear it's a plot against you.

I couldn't think of any reason someone would take a power cord and not the laptop.

Unless the cord had been used to strangle someone.

I wished I could go back to not thinking of a reason. But why hit someone on the head with a rock and then strangle them? I mean, why do either? But even if I had a reason to believe someone got hit on the head with the fluorite, that didn't mean they'd also strangled someone, or that another random person had strangled someone. I needed actual clues, not panicked wild guesses because I was nervous, and my imagination was running away with me.

Okay. So, if I jumped way back from that conclusion and used logic, what did I find? The cord was missing. Maybe Shelley had found it when she cleaned and had donated it or threw it away. A rational, likely possibility. Unfortunately, it didn't get me closer to breaking into Reggie's computer.

Next I browsed through the filing cabinets. It would take days to go through every folder, so I just checked the titles, hoping I'd come across something with a helpful label such as WHY SOMEONE WANTS TO KILL ME.

No such luck. I did find out that Reggie, or someone who'd handled the files before him, or a whole string of people over the years, had been terrible at alphabetizing. That wasn't psychometry, just observation. I put reorganization on my to-do list, but way at the bottom, after unpacking, learning my way around town, investigating a murder, and dealing with the new donation.

Maybe that's why no one prior to me had gotten around to fixing the filing system. I could easily envision years passing without that chore getting to the top of my priorities.

I couldn't find a folder on the fluorite. Did that mean

the mineral itself was important in all this, so much so that someone took the folder? Or just that the filing system was messed up? Or maybe it was part of a donated collection in a folder listed by the donor's name, in which case it might take months to track it down. The fluorite had a number on the bottom, but I hadn't yet found a master document that explained how the numbers related to the files—optimistically assuming that they did.

Surely someone in the throes of violent conflict wouldn't bother to grab a particular mineral sample as their weapon. Fluorite wasn't even very hard. If you wanted to do damage, you'd be better off with granite. Granted, the one sample of granite in the office sat on the floor and probably weighed over twenty pounds. Your victim might escape while you tried to heft the rock. In any case, while I didn't entirely dismiss the importance of the weapon being fluorite, it was probably random: The attacker had grabbed something convenient. (That was also a good excuse not to spend the time searching the files for info on the fluorite.)

If the office held any clues, I'd failed to recognize them. At least it was cleaner, and I'd boxed up most of the things Reggie might have handled extensively.

The laptop seemed a better bet for finding out about Reggie Heap. I needed that cord. I could order one online, but that might take several days to arrive, and I doubted Bonneville had an appropriate store. Maybe the museum had extra cords in the office.

The laptop was pretty standard for an older style, but it had some wear marks. I didn't want to risk someone recognizing it as Reggie's, so I couldn't show it as I asked for spare cords. Plus I didn't want to handle it, and it would seem weird to carry a laptop around in a towel. I studied the plug hole to determine what kind of cord would fit.

It was almost five. The museum was open from ten to six, so I had another hour before quitting time. I had gathered a box of what I assumed were Reggie's personal items: an old windbreaker, a small vase that had held pens and pencils, and a few other things I didn't want in my office.

Unfortunately, I couldn't get rid of them quite yet. I needed to know if they'd tell me anything about Reggie.

The exhibit room was empty. I sat at the desk and took off my gloves. I ran my hands over the windbreaker and got a sense of annoyance, which would fit with something he kept around in case of unexpected rain. I touched the coffee mug warily but only got vague distraction and a desire for coffee. That was the most relatable glimpse of Reggie so far. The pens, pencils, and half bag of candy said nothing useful and could go in the trash, along with the paper clips and rubber bands. They might still be usable, but I preferred a fresh start.

And yes, I was cleaning up a crime scene, but I could hardly cordon it off and call a CSI team. At least I wasn't cleaning the carpet. It didn't look bloodstained, but the carpet was a mottled brown and tan to begin with, ugly but good for hiding dirt, spilled coffee, and evidence of gruesome crimes.

I scowled at the vase. It looked handmade, but not very well, like a child's art project or a beginning potter's work. It seemed the most dangerous item, for my particular brand of danger. A handmade item could have the emotions of the original maker. It also might elicit strong emotions from someone who'd gotten it as a gift. On the other hand, it wasn't likely Reggie had touched the vase a lot, let alone held it in his hands while he felt strongly about things. It might have been sitting on the desk for years, holding pens and pencils as any emotional echoes faded.

It was probably safe enough to touch. But my hands and arms and shoulders ached. My head throbbed dully. I wanted to learn something, but I hoped I wouldn't feel anything.

I braced my elbows on the desk, breathed deeply, and slid my fingers around the vase.

The memories were distant. The faintest sense of small hands looping coils of clay, smoothing it, glazing it. Not a child's hands, but an adolescent's or petite woman's. What else? Happiness, but also a touch of nerves? Someone new gripping the vase. Interest, but not in the vase itself. Intense focus on a person. Lust?

It was all too faint and remote and muddled. I couldn't even guess if the second person had been Reggie or someone else. And it hardly mattered. If it had been Reggie, he might've been attracted to the person who made the vase—or someone else who'd sold it, or someone who was around when he was holding it.

So I'd learned next to nothing, but I hadn't been zapped with horrible memories. I'd call that a win. That's the advantage of wanting two opposing things: I'd probably get one of them.

I put the vase back in the box and glanced toward the door. Kit stood on the other side, smirking, his brow furrowed. How long had he been watching?

I stood up, waving him in.

He opened the door. "Didn't mean to disturb you. I'm just walking through the museum to let people know we're closing in ten minutes. Lock the door to this room behind you when you leave so no one can wander in right after I cleared a section."

"Okay, makes sense. I need to drop some things off at the front office, so I'll head out now." I grabbed my backpack and the box of Reggie's stuff.

"Want me to carry that for you?"

"I have it. You can finish your rounds." I locked the office door behind me.

We walked through the geology room. "How was your first day? I hope we didn't scare you off." Kit grinned, playing the part of a charming rogue.

"It was fine. There's a lot to learn. And my stuff is coming soon, so I'll be really busy for a few weeks." I yawned.

"It's going to take me a while to recover from driving out here too."

It was a broad hint to leave me alone, but I suspected he wouldn't take a narrow hint.

"You might be feeling the altitude as well," Kit said. "We're at four thousand feet elevation. It's a lot drier than where you were too. Drink at least twice the water you think you need."

"Right. Good point." That was actually helpful. I felt bad for suspecting the worst of him. "Thank you."

"I aim to please. Don't forget to lock up." He winked, gave a cheery wave, and headed down the hallway to . . . I had no idea where what was in that direction.

I locked the door to the geology wing and headed toward the museum entrance. I somehow wound up in a section I hadn't seen yet, a hallway with small rooms or alcoves on each side. On my right, they were decorated as rooms from different eras. An old trading post. A homesteader's cabin, with a handmade quilt on the narrow bed, wooden furniture, and food that I hoped was fake. The inside of a mine, with rough rock walls and a mannequin wearing overalls and an old headlamp, holding a pick. A sign said that one was based on when they'd mined guano—bat poop used for fertilizer—at Carlsbad Caverns.

Those rooms were roped off, but on the other side, people could go take pictures with two aliens and a spaceship, some dinosaur sculptures locked in battle (each one taller than a person but not the size of the actual T-Rex or triceratops), and wooden cutouts of gunslingers. It seemed a little silly, but also smart. If people took pictures and posted them online, that promoted the museum.

I finally found the front counter where they took money for the museum and gift shop. I hadn't yet met the young man behind it.

"Hi," I said. "I'm Petra, the new employee in the geology wing."

"I'm Austin. I work here." His friendly smile showed crooked teeth.

I smiled back. "I guessed. Are you here every day?" He looked to be in his teens, tall and skinny and not yet filled out. He seemed like he should still be in school.

"No, I'm a senior, but I only have to take four classes this semester, so I work here most afternoons. Saving money for college."

"Good for you."

The museum had a small office behind the front counter. A tiny woman with permed white hair came out the open door.

"Petra? I'm Mrs. Banditt. Call me Gloria." She held out a hand.

I shifted the box to one arm in order to shake her hand and realized I still had the white gloves on, although they weren't so white anymore. "Oh, sorry. I've been cleaning."

"I suppose it needed it. I doubt Reggie cleaned the place

the whole time he was here." She shook her head. "Men."

"I have this box of his stuff." I set it on the counter. "Peyton told me to bring it by and you'd sort out what to do with it."

She and the boy both peered into the box. "Austin, put that on the desk for Mr. Banditt," Gloria said. He carried it into the office.

"Oh, do you have any spare laptop cords?" I asked. "Mine is probably in one of the boxes that's coming later this week."

"Austin, grab the lost and found box."

He crouched, pulled a box from under the counter, and set it in front of me. Mrs. Banditt went back to the office as I shuffled through the box with my gloved hand. Sunglasses, a scarf, several single gloves, and even a ring, but no laptop cords.

"Well, it was a long shot," I said. "I guess people don't bring their laptops to tour a museum."

"What kind of cord do you need?" Austin asked. "If mine fits, I can lend it to you for a couple of days."

I described it.

"Oh, that's kind of an old style, I think."

"Yeah, it's an old laptop. You know a lot about computers?"

He nodded. "I did the website for my family's ranch. I'll go to college for animal husbandry, but I want to get a minor in computer sciences."

That was handy. If I couldn't get into the laptop myself, maybe Austin would know some tricks. But that would mean explaining the situation, or coming up with a plausible lie for why I didn't know my own password.

"Well, thanks anyway," I said.

"You should ask Haven." Austin got a dreamy look.

"She has an old laptop?" She wasn't too many years older than Austin.

"She handles the twentieth century collection."

"Oh, right. I doubt this laptop is *that* old." I winced. I would surely know how old my own laptop was. But he didn't notice, his mind apparently still on Haven. "But I'll ask her anyway. Do you know if she's still here?"

"I haven't seen her leave."

"Okay, thanks." I was starting to hate Reggie Heap. Not only did he get himself killed—possibly, unless I was completely misreading everything—and dump the situation in my lap, but he was making me act sociable with people. What a monster.

But he probably didn't deserve to die.

## Chapter Seven

IT HAD ALREADY been a very long day. But Austin showed me where Haven's office was on a museum map, and I headed back there. The map looked like a particularly dense hidden picture puzzle, but maybe if I studied it for an hour or ten it would start to make sense.

I entered the room that had artifacts from Old West outlaws and lawmen as Haven came through the door on the opposite side. She wore a light jacket and a cross-body bag decorated with bright orange and yellow flowers. "Hey, Petra! Are you checking out the displays or are you lost?" She pulled the door closed behind her.

"I was actually looking for you. Sorry, this can wait until tomorrow. I just need to borrow a laptop cord. Austin said you might have something."

"Sure." She pushed the door open again and bounced back the way she'd come. The next room, or rather hallway, had floor-to-ceiling glass cases along each wall, one with rows of little toy cars and the other with baby dolls. The dolls weren't labeled as possessed, but they sure looked creepy enough. Some had unnerving stairs, others had drooping eyelids and cheeks that look bloated, and many had fine cracks across the porcelain faces.

Haven unlocked a door from the middle of the hallway, which led into another small room. How did this museum even fit all these rooms together? Maybe the Roswell alien crash was real after all, and the museum had snagged some alien technology.

The room was about twelve by twelve, crammed with desks, each holding multiple computers. The old monitors had words on the screens, as if awake and in use, but they were actually stick-on labels with the history of that computer model.

"Do you think any of these will work? If not, we can look through the boxes. I might even have a universal power cord set." Haven gestured to boxes stuffed under the desks. "You would not believe all the old junk people give us. Like we really need more than one Apple One computer! But Peyton doesn't like to turn down anything. He's afraid people will stop donating if they think the museum won't keep their rubbish."

That explained a lot. I leaned over the desk with more recent computers, from the last decade or so. "Maybe that one." I pointed.

"You can take it home and check."

"Really? I can take part of the museum display?"

"They'll function just as well whether or not they have cords, especially since they aren't actually plugged in. But I thought it was interesting how the cords changed along with the other technology."

Spoken like a true museum curator. I reached around to unplug the cord. It looked like the right type and size.

"I'll check right now." I slid my backpack off my shoulders and crouched next to it on the floor. I tried the cord without taking the laptop out of my pack. It was a little awkward, but Haven might think I was just lazy. Or she might not think anything at all, since she pulled out her phone.

"It fits." I shoved the cord into my pack. "Thanks."

"Wait until it actually works. It's probably beyond its life expectancy, so I can't guarantee anything." She hesitated. "Do you want to power on now and make sure?" She didn't sound enthusiastic, which was great because she wouldn't wonder why I turned down that very sensible offer.

"I won't keep you any longer. If it doesn't work I'll check back tomorrow."

She brightened. "Sounds good."

We left the room. Haven pulled the door closed and locked it. Her key ring must have had a dozen regular keys, plus twenty or thirty tiny ones. I frowned.

She glanced over at me. "What's up?"

"I have keys to my office and the main geology room, and Peyton said he'd get me a storeroom key. But I just realized I don't have keys to the display cases in my department."

"They're not in Reggie's office? I mean, your office? I like to keep all my keys together, but he might have only carried the room keys and left the case keys in his desk."

"I've cleaned the place pretty thoroughly and haven't found them."

Her eyes opened wide. "Really? That's weird. I hope Reggie didn't lose them before he died."

Hm. Lost, or stolen? I hadn't noticed anything obviously missing from the display cases, but items might have been removed and replaced with less valuable minerals, or the remaining objects shuffled around so gaps were hidden. With Reggie dead, probably no one else at the museum would notice changes like that, and I wouldn't figure it out unless I went through all the files, and not even then if some had been removed or if records weren't kept well.

It seemed awfully complicated. If someone wanted to steal minerals, why not grab them and run? Were any of the samples unique enough to attract notice if they were reported stolen? That would make selling them harder.

"How likely is it that Reggie would lose the keys?" I asked.

She shrugged. "I wouldn't put it past him. Anything that makes life harder for other people."

"Oh?" *Gimme that insight into Reggie Heap.*

Her shoulders hunched. "He's gone. I shouldn't bad-mouth him now."

*Yes you should.* But I couldn't explain why I wanted gossip. I was tired and my head hurt, and I still had to try breaking into a computer, and I wanted to be home with my animals.

I let it go. "I'll ask Peyton about the keys tomorrow. Maybe he just forgot to give them to me. If they're really gone, I guess we'll have to call a locksmith."

"I'm not sure we have a locksmith in town."

"Well, I'm not planning to change displays immediately. It'll take time to learn what's there now and go through the new donation in the storeroom."

"Yeah. Sorry things aren't more organized for you." She didn't sound surprised about it though.

We headed back through the outlaw room. Haven paused to lock that door behind her. That could have been my chance to skedaddle, but that seemed rude when she'd just done me a favor. In any case, given her high energy level and my fatigue, she'd probably catch up with me.

As we headed toward the museum entrance, Haven said, "By the way, don't feel like you have to work *too* hard."

"Oh?" I was saying that a lot, wasn't I?

"I'm not saying you should do nothing! But you could hardly do worse than Reggie, and this place is pretty easy-going. Peyton has big dreams and all, but we're in the middle of nowhere. This is never going to be The Met. It's okay to work at your own pace. When Peyton gets overzealous, Gloria reels him in."

"Thanks for the tip. Is that why you're here? The easier pace?"

She didn't answer as we passed the front counter and

waved to Austin. We stepped outside and I understood why Haven wore a jacket, even though it had been fairly warm when I went home for lunch. With the sun lower, the temperature had dropped noticeably.

"I have plans, but this place will do for now. Well, see you tomorrow!" She strode down the street.

I turned to my van. It was tempting to go straight home, but I really needed groceries.

The store was modest in size but had all the basics, if not all the specialty items people in big cities might now expect. Fortunately I didn't need gluten-free products or alternatives to dairy, and I couldn't afford fancy items such as kumquats or durian fruit even if I found them. The pet food aisle had cat food, dog food, and birdseed, but only a few choices, and not the higher quality options that were best for animal health. I'd add cat food to my online order of ferret, guinea pig, and rat food. I grabbed enough human food for a week and some cat food the felines would probably enjoy so much they'd never want to go back to the healthy stuff.

I was famished and exhausted by the time I got home, but thanks to the short commute, it was only seven p.m. I quickly fed the cats. The smaller animals had food available all the time, so topping off their dishes and giving them fresh water could wait until I'd fed myself. I opened a can of soup, realized the kitchen didn't have a microwave, and found a pot I could use on the stove. While the soup heated, I plugged in the laptop so it could start charging. I also spread some of the animals' blankets across the couch so I wouldn't have to touch Reggie's furniture.

As I settled in with my soup, the cats joined me, even Onyx. While I ate, I searched for "how to break into a laptop" on my phone. I wasn't surprised to find plenty of information and was even less surprised that it got complicated. The simplest way was to request a reset by answering security questions, but I wasn't likely to know those answers. Or I could take the laptop back to factory reset, which I'd want to do if I was keeping it for my own use. But first I wanted to learn more about Reggie, like why he might have been a victim of violence, so I had to get in without erasing anything.

Some methods depended on the computer having a certain operating system, and I didn't know what was on this laptop. Other options required a special reset disk or a bootable flash drive, which I could order but it would take a couple of days.

I could wait. Reggie had been dead two weeks already. I was so tired, I wouldn't have the energy to do anything with his laptop that evening even if I managed to break in. I had plenty to keep me busy for a few days (weeks, months).

But I worried about taking over Reggie's job, his house, a good chunk of his life. He was dead, and someone had been seriously injured or killed in his office, not too long ago. It was hard to believe those things weren't related. Had Reggie caught a thief at work, and the thief killed him? Had the confrontation been personal, not directly connected to the museum? No one seemed to like Reggie all that much, but they didn't seem to hate him either. Indifference usually didn't lead to violence. If he'd been killed because of something happening at the museum, it might be over—but if it wasn't, I was now in Reggie's place.

I needed to know more about Reggie, what valuables the museum had and how they secured them, and probably a bunch of other things I hadn't thought of yet. Once I figured out what had happened in that office, I could get back to my regular life. Or my irregular life, as the case might be.

Apparently you could actually copy someone's fingerprints to get past a fingerprint scanner. I could probably find Reggie's fingerprints somewhere, maybe even on the laptop itself. But then I'd need to get a decent picture of the print, create a negative of the image, print the result, and put wood glue on top of the imitated fingerprint.

Also, this laptop didn't have a fingerprint scanner. I'd wasted time on that tangent, which showed how tired I was. Or maybe I was so far outside my field that I would've made the mistake anyway. My knowledge of criminal investigation came from watching CSI shows with ridiculously advanced technology or British mysteries where lovable vicars or nuns used their life experience to solve bizarre crimes. That was hardly accurate investigative training, and I'd mostly had the shows on as background noise while I studied.

Basically, all the options seemed to be beyond my technology skills or to require equipment I didn't have. I still had an option that wouldn't be mentioned online. I groaned. Amber paused in grooming her back leg to cock her head at me.

"Stand by," I said. "I might need your therapy expertise in a minute."

I picked up the laptop, still using the towel, and set it on the couch. I turned and sat cross-legged so the laptop was in front of me and I was supported by an armrest and the back of the couch. I used a corner of a blanket to open the laptop. It appeared to be charging, so that was good news.

I hovered my hands over the keyboard. "Come on," I muttered, "get it over with."

Amber squeezed past the laptop and sniffed at it. She touched the keyboard with a paw, which brought up the password screen. I scooped the cat onto my lap so she wouldn't interfere with my work. Besides, her warmth was comforting.

I rested my fingertips on the keyboard, in standard typing position, and closed my eyes. Impressions swirled through my mind.

*Anticipation. Greed?*

He was looking forward to something, a fairly strong emotion so it was either recent or ongoing. At a guess, I'd say recent. He wanted something and thought he was about to get it.

But what about the password? I skimmed my fingers over

the keys. If his password was a random string of letters, numbers, and symbols, I'd never get it this way. If it was a few words that had little meaning to him, my chances were slim. I needed emotion. But if the password was important, meaningful, something that got a reaction from Reggie Heap every time he typed it . . .

*Amusement. Snickering at his own humor. Feeling a bit naughty.*

I opened my eyes and typed in *schisthappens*. It was an old geology joke. Schist is a fairly common metamorphic rock. It's gray and not that exciting, except to geologists with the sense of humor of a twelve-year-old boy. Then you get all kinds of jokes, such as SCHIST HAPPENS, METAMORPHICALLY SPEAKING, which I'd seen on T-shirts.

I hit Enter. The computer flashed "password incorrect."

Schist. I'd been ninety percent sure I had it right. But did he have a different kind of schist joke, or something added on to what I already had? *I don't give a schist*, or *no schist*, or *geologists know their schist*? None of those felt quite right.

Amber twisted in my lap, purring. I rubbed her cheek while I thought. If I tried too many incorrect passwords, the computer might lock me out. Not to mention I was already aching and queasy from everything I'd done that day.

I flexed my hands a few times and typed *SchistHappens*. I hit Enter.

I was in.

# Chapter Eight

I WAS IN the computer but out of energy. I could have fallen asleep immediately, but I had to care for my pets. Since I was forced to get up for that, I managed to brush my teeth, wash my face, and moisturize. My skin felt dry, my lips chapped. Right, drink more water.

I slept on the couch, despite the risk that the blankets covering it could be disturbed by me turning over—or by the cats deciding to have a wrestling match at three a.m. If that happened and I wound up touching the couch surface, I might pick up sensations and have weird dreams. My dreams are pretty weird anyway, so it seemed worth the risk. My shoulder and hip still hurt from a night on the wooden floor with only blankets for cushioning.

I got through the night. If I had disturbing couch-influenced dreams, I didn't remember them. Maybe I was distracted by Jet attacking my feet every time I moved them. Or by Amber snuggling my entire face. Not to mention the strange sounds outside the house. No traffic noise, horns honking, or sirens. But I heard coyotes! Either that or ghosts. Onyx burrowed under the blanket with me, trembling, which doesn't provide evidence either way. The birds also started a racket at dawn, which was far earlier than I needed to get up. At least Amber and Jet got off me so they could exchange insults with their feathered frenemies through the windows.

I hadn't bothered to set an alarm, because I didn't have to be at work until ten a.m. Also because I'd forgotten. But by the time I dragged myself out of bed, stumbled through showering and dressing, took care of the animals, and gulped some peanut butter toast, I had to leave. I shoved Reggie's laptop into my backpack, made sure I had my keys, and kissed the cats goodbye. Shelley was in her garden but facing the other way. I crept past so as not to get caught in conversation.

I made it to the museum at five minutes to ten. The door was locked, and I didn't have an outside door key. I peered through the glass, saw someone behind the counter, and knocked. Gloria Banditt came around to open the door for me.

"Good morning, dear. The others are in the break room."

"Break room?"

She gestured down a hall between the gift shop and the head office/front counter. "The door at the end."

I hesitated. If everyone was in the break room, I could sneak back to my office without having to speak to anyone. But if *everyone* was there, maybe I was supposed to be there too.

"Is it a meeting?" I asked.

"Nothing so official, but the staff tends to gather there first thing. Peyton likes to check in with everyone, make sure things are going well." Gloria smiled softly, indulgent and amused. "I think everyone else just likes to get their coffee and put off starting work for a few more minutes. We rarely get visitors right at opening, but if we do and they want a tour, I call Kit up to take them through."

So they locked the individual sections of the museum at night but let tourists wander at will through the empty building during the day.

"What about security?" I asked. "Most of the things in my area are in locked glass cases or are too big and heavy to slip under your coat and carry out. I guess that's true for most of the museum, but . . ." I trailed off, not wanting to be critical, but many portable objects sat around, such as the smaller items in the rooms set up to look like historic cabins or whatever.

"We've rarely had a problem." She chuckled. "Or if we have, we haven't noticed, with so much in here. But anything really valuable is kept secure, and we do have cameras."

That would make it harder for anyone to sneak around at night. It might also mean a recording of my odd behavior in Reggie's office.

I tried to sound casual. "In every room? How are they monitored?"

Gloria leaned forward and whispered, "I'll tell you a secret. Not all the cameras work. They're more of a deterrent, so people *think* we're watching. We do have some that start recording when anything moves. One covers the back of the museum. Two are up here, covering the front door, cash register, and gift shop. And there's a real camera in the room with the outlaws and lawman exhibits, since that's what we're famous for. The recordings are kept for a week, so we can check if something is missing or there are signs of a break-in, but no one wants to waste time reviewing footage of cats and raccoons in the yard."

Good for me, that no one saw me practically pass out from touching the murder rock. Less good for the museum if someone snuck in and stole something more than a week ago, and no one had noticed it missing. Reggie wouldn't have, being dead. Given what I'd heard, he might not have noticed missing minerals when he was alive.

The other curators might know their areas well enough to spot a change, especially if the item was large or featured on the tours. I was still skeptical that anyone would notice if someone had, say, removed a few toys and slid the others over to fill the gap. But an item would have to be really valuable to make that kind of theft worthwhile.

Could the museum have valuable items and not know it? Something Peyton collected fifty years ago might be a sought-after antique now.

I kept those thoughts to myself. "I guess I'll stop in the

break room. Thanks for the info. Oh—one other thing. I don't have the keys to the cases in the rocks and minerals wing. Do you have them?"

Her eyebrows went up. "I don't think so. One moment." She retreated to the office and came back shaking her head. "There's nothing on the key rack. We keep duplicate keys for all the doors, but not for the individual cases. If Peyton didn't give you Reggie's keys, I'd expect them to be in his office. Or *your* office now! We're so glad to have you."

"Thanks. It's nice to be here." I headed to the break room.

I took a deep breath before pushing open the door marked PRIVATE. I scanned the room to get my bearings. Peyton was holding forth on some subject, swinging his hands as if conducting an orchestra. Kit leaned against the counter looking bored as he sipped from a big white mug with a WANTED poster design. Haven stirred something into her coffee as she watched Peyton, looking amused.

Liberty sat at a table and was the first to glance over at me. She smiled and waved me into the room. Haven's glance followed the gesture to me, and she grinned.

I got a weird feeling. Like . . . people were happy to see me? And I enjoyed it?

I liked Haven and Liberty. I might enjoy being friends with them—assuming, of course, neither of them were murderers. But even taking murder out of the equation, friendship was hard with a secret like mine. When did you tell people? How would they react? But maybe if we got to know each other as coworkers . . .

"Petra!" Peyton exclaimed. "Come in, my dear. Did I forget to show you the break room yesterday? I fear I might have."

"The most important room in the museum." Kit winked at me.

It was nice to be welcomed, but it also made me extremely self-conscious. "Gloria pointed me this way. Good thing, because I didn't have time to stop for coffee, and my coffee maker is still somewhere between here and Seattle." Was that a normal thing to say? I felt like I was in a play but didn't have the script.

"We all have our favorite mugs," Liberty said. "Those are usually in the draining rack, because we never get around to putting them away. There are plenty of others in the cupboard above the sink."

I found a mug that was purple, my favorite color, and even better, it was enormous. As I filled it I noticed the hot air balloon design, which was pretty, but the words I GOT HIGH IN NEW MEXICO might not make the best first impressions. Switching would just call attention to it though.

I tried to think of something to say. "I didn't mean to interrupt," I told Peyton.

"No matter." He glanced at his watch. "The museum is officially open now, so I'm sure everyone wants to race off and get to work."

That was apparently a joke, since no one moved except to drink their coffee.

I cleared my throat. "By the way, I don't have the keys to the cases in my department. I haven't found them in Reggie's office, and Gloria said they aren't in the main office."

Peyton's bushy eyebrows drew together. "Really? I assumed Reggie left them in his office. The sheriff only gave me back the door keys."

"The—oh, you mean after . . ." I trailed off.

Peyton nodded. "After the crash."

I felt queasy. I'd been cautious with the keys at first, worried that if my predecessor kept them on his person all day long, they'd pick up on a lot of sensations. Apparently they had been with him when he died. And yet, the keys had been fairly quiet. Maybe he only touched them when he unlocked doors and didn't have strong feelings about them.

Or given what I'd heard about Reggie, maybe he didn't bother locking the doors, so he didn't always carry the keys.

"He had a separate key ring for the case keys," Kit said.

"It's possible those are still in the car," Peyton said. "It was in pretty bad shape, having run off the road like that. I heard the tow truck had a hard time getting his car back up the slope."

That didn't do anything for my queasiness, but I managed to ask, "Where did it happen?" Everyone looked at me, and my face went hot. "Most of what I've seen around here is pretty flat. Like you'd run off the road and just be, you know, at the edge of the road."

"Head north and you hit some mountains," Liberty said. "What he was doing out there is a mystery. I never heard of Reggie hiking."

"Just going for a drive, maybe," Kit said. "But he probably didn't take the case keys with him. Why would he?"

"If they aren't in his office, perhaps he left them at his house," Peyton said. "But Shelley would have told me if she'd found them."

"She didn't say anything to me either," I said. "And I've looked through the house pretty well. It's not like I need those keys immediately, but . . ."

"I'm sure they'll turn up," Peyton said. "Maybe in the workshop? Reggie could be a little absent-minded. I didn't notice them, but we weren't looking for keys."

"Okay." Missing keys sounded like a big deal to me, but apparently not to the museum. If the keys didn't turn up in a few days, I'd ask about a locksmith so I could start reorganizing the displays.

But what had happened to those keys? Reggie might have lost them months ago and not told anyone. They might be in the wrecked car, hidden somewhere inaccessible. It wasn't necessarily a big mystery or part of some nefarious plot. Still. We had missing keys, a dead man, a hidden laptop, and a rock used as a weapon. Were they all connected?

I sipped my coffee and half listened to Peyton nag Kit about repainting the photo cutout boards. That was apparently the name for the painted boards that had holes for people to put their faces through and take pictures. I remembered two in front of the museum painted like a gunslinger and sheriff, so people could take pictures with their faces on the painted bodies, looking like they were about to shoot each other. I guess violence is charming when it's historical.

Liberty rinsed her mug and put it in the dish drying rack. "Well, I'm off to my lair." She gave me a look that I interpreted as an invitation to escape along with her.

I joined her at the door. "Er, is it okay if I take my coffee through the museum?" A sign on the main door said no food or drink except water, but I wasn't sure if that applied to us.

"Yeah." When the door closed behind us, she added, "I have a kettle in my office, and a wide selection of tea, if you ever fancy a cup. You may have noticed that the coffee in the break room isn't great. Kit and Peyton can't tell the difference, and Haven drinks it because it's free. I bring my own tea bags and have a mug there to be sociable. You can grab coffee to take to your office, or bring your own setup."

"Thanks." We passed the front counter, waving to Gloria in the office. "I appreciate your guidance. It's a little overwhelming." Especially with the possible murder, I didn't add.

"I'm sure."

We paused by a display of old WANTED posters, where I would go left. She studied me intently for a few seconds. I had no idea what she was looking for, or what she saw.

Finally she said, "You'll be fine. Before you know it, this will feel like home. You fit." She turned and headed to her domain.

Had that been a compliment or an insult?

# Chapter Nine

I GOT BACK to my office. Despite what had happened there, I felt safe with the door closed. That was an illusion. Maybe Reggie had felt safe too. But at least I didn't have to come up with things to say and then wonder why I'd said them.

I enjoyed the bit of privacy for almost a minute before the questions flooded me. Most of all, *Now what?*

I thought I could enjoy working at the museum, so I ought to get started on my actual job and maybe even make some social connections so my coworkers didn't think I was a complete misanthrope. But until I knew the truth about Reggie's death, I couldn't trust anyone, and if I kept cleaning and organizing, I might destroy evidence that I could use to get the police involved in the future.

I pulled out the laptop, hoping it would tell me *something* useful, and typed in the password. I started with his email, but he didn't seem to use it much. I didn't see anything suspicious skimming through emails he'd received the week before he died. Most of the message headings sound like spam. I checked a few to make sure they weren't personal messages disguised by a spam subject line, but no, the email with the subject line "learn mind tricks to get swedishh supermodels into bed" was just selling some ridiculous product. I even copied a few links in case they redirected me to a private message board or something. Nope. I made a hasty exit.

I moved on to files saved on his computer. It didn't take long to learn why Reggie had that sense of anticipation when he got on his computer. I checked the last two videos he'd opened. A few seconds were enough to confirm the titles were accurate. I wasn't about to watch *Teen Girls XXX* in case of hidden messages partway through. I closed the laptop, feeling slightly queasy.

So I had learned something about Reggie Heap. I try not to be judgmental about what people want to do with their bodies, either alone or with other consenting adults, as long as they don't insist on telling me about it. But the video titles suggested Reggie was interested in girls who were teenagers or preteens. Watching the videos was bad enough. People who were willing to pay for those videos or find them on ad-filled websites encouraged the exploitation of kids.

But had Reggie been involved in something even worse? Had he assaulted a local girl, or paid one for sex, and her family found out? Had he been involved in sex trafficking? A town this size surely didn't have brothels that catered to specific tastes, but we were only a few hours from the Mexico border. Had he driven down there and gotten in trouble?

But in that case, he would have died in Mexico. I couldn't imagine a pimp or someone involved in a human trafficking ring bothering to set up a murder to look like an accidental death.

So what should I do about what I'd found? I doubted the local police could stop or arrest the people making the videos, even if they cared. Reggie was dead. He couldn't be punished much more. If he'd been killed by an angry young woman, or her angry family, I had some sympathy. But did I have enough sympathy to let them get away with murder?

I didn't want a computer full of child porn in my possession, even though the email account would show it was really Reggie's. I needed to either destroy it, wipe it clean, or give it to the authorities. If I did one of the first two, it prevented me from ever doing the third.

To put off making a decision, I did another thorough hunt for the missing keys. When I didn't find them in the office, I searched the rocks and minerals hall in case Reggie had dropped them or left them on a shelf. It was a big room, around fifty by thirty feet, with dozens of cases. Plenty of pretty rocks to catch the eye, so the key ring might go unnoticed, especially if the museum had kept the room locked from Reggie's death until I arrived.

While I was at it, I looked for anything suspicious. Empty spots in the cases. Dust showing where things had been moved to cover up an item's absence. I didn't find any of that, but I got better acquainted with the exhibits. They were varied, fairly interesting, and probably worth many thousands of dollars all together. Individual pieces were worth anything from nothing to a couple thousand if you could find the right buyer.

Several small tourist groups came through. I smiled and said, "Welcome," so they'd know I worked there in case they had questions—or wondered why I was crouching to look under cases and stretching to see the tops of shelves. Most didn't stay long. Maybe my behavior made them nervous. Or they were anxious to get back on the road or just not interested in rocks, the arsenolites. (Arsenolite is an arsenic mineral and a pretty good insult, if you're a geologist.)

I went back to the office to think about what I'd learned. One, the place needed a good cleaning. I didn't know if that was Reggie's job—my job now—or if they had a cleaning crew that either wasn't earning their money or wasn't getting paid enough to make it all the way back there.

This wing definitely seemed neglected. Maybe Peyton had been slightly relieved to get rid of Reggie without having to fire him. On the other hand, I doubted my section brought any money into the museum. They could probably close it up and no one would notice or care. Peyton wanted to be remembered. Was that enough to explain his goal of building up the geology displays? Had he decided that outlaws and aliens were frivolous, but a world-class mineral museum could be his legacy?

I had no idea. I wasn't normally suspicious of everyone's

reasons for everything, and I wasn't exactly the person to ask if behaviors were normal and sensible. But I did know *normal* and *sensible* were often not the same thing, and many people *weren't* rational, unfortunately, since I couldn't figure out whether anyone's behavior made sense, especially in such a different community from what I had known.

My investigations and pondering had taken me nearly to one. Decision time. I no longer wanted to keep the computer for my own use or even touch it again. I could stick in it the drawer and ignore it, hand it over to Peyton without mentioning what I'd found, or take it to the police with an explanation.

If I took the computer to the police, I could ask about Reggie's accident. Maybe it wouldn't even seem too weird that I was interested.

I used my phone to search for the local police station. Turned out we had both police and a sheriff. What was the difference? The internet informed me that sheriffs were often elected while police officers were hired by the city. But which did I want? Had Peyton mentioned the sheriff when talking about keys? I hadn't paid close enough attention.

Okay, I'd been meaning to look for any report on Reggie's death anyway. I found a brief mention of the *accident* that quoted the sheriff. So sheriff it was. The report didn't tell me anything else new, although it identified the mountain road where he was found, including the mile marker. While I was at it, I checked for any news of dead bodies or mysterious head injuries for the last two weeks. Nothing. While that didn't *confirm* my suspicion that Reggie was the victim, it seemed to narrow the field a bit. Surely in a town this small, people couldn't go missing without anyone noticing, or get injured without it being reported.

I locked my office and slipped out the back door to avoid any more lunch invitations. The sheriff's office was only a few blocks away, but the eight-minute walk was long enough for my nerves to start buzzing. Most people avoid law enforcement, I guess. Even those who assume the police are honest and trustworthy get nervous when cops are around, like they're afraid the police will catch them at something, even if they're not doing anything wrong.

It's worse when you have secrets. I'd always avoided law enforcement on general principle. Given how my own family and friends reacted to my psychic ability, I wasn't about to share it with strangers.

I didn't want to tell anyone about my psychometry, so I couldn't say I suspected Reggie Heap had been murdered in the office I now had. I'd focus on the laptop, and my concern as a good citizen that I should report what I'd found. Maybe then I could slide in some questions about Reggie's death. Was it considered suspicious? If not, could I nudge them that way? That was my main goal. It would be nice to think the authorities would do something about porn featuring underage girls, but you may have noticed I'm not an optimist.

By the time I found the sheriff's office, I was lightheaded and had to keep reminding myself to breathe. I pushed open the door and stepped into an odd feeling of déjà vu. The room looked like it belonged in the museum: model of Wild West Sheriff's Office. Wooden floors, stucco walls, a potbellied stove, and two actual jail cells with bars.

A woman sat behind an old wooden desk with the one jarring modern note, a computer. Actually, she was a modern note as well. First of all, they probably didn't have women working at the jails back in the day. If they had, they wouldn't have looked like this one, in her low-cut paisley blouse and drop earrings with alternating turquoise and silver beads. She was plump, with a cheerful, round face, maroon lipstick, and penciled eyebrows. Her dark hair was pulled back in a bun held in place with two chopsticks. She didn't look more than twenty.

She beamed at me. "Good morning."

"Um. Hi." I looked over at the jail cells with their iron bars and old-fashioned locks. "This is an actual sheriff's office, right, not a historical site?"

She laughed, high-pitched and loud. "It's both. It was the old jail. They decided to keep this as the front room of the sheriff's office." She jerked a thumb toward the door behind her. "It's more modern back there, don't worry. Now, can I help you?"

The words I'd practiced had fled. "It's complicated."

She studied my face. "Are you . . . injured? Do you need

a doctor?"

"No, I'm fine. It's not that." I assumed she was asking if I'd been assaulted. That probably said something about how flustered I looked. "I found something I thought I should turn over to the police. Or the sheriff. Maybe you can't do anything, but I didn't feel right keeping this to myself." I laughed awkwardly. "Like I said, it's complicated. I'd rather not have to explain twice, if you don't mind."

"Okay, let me call someone. Have a seat." She picked up her cell phone.

The wooden chairs along the wall looked even less comfortable than the jail cells. I was too jittery to sit anyway. I eased over to a large bulletin board on the wall, hung with a dozen WANTED posters. That was another weird echo of all the Wild West WANTED posters at the museum. Most of these seemed to be for people who'd committed crimes several years ago, though not as far back as Billy the Kid. I stared at them, not really focusing.

"Someone will be with you in a minute," the young woman said behind me.

"Thanks." I kept looking at the posters. Mainly it was something to do, as I didn't really expect to run into any of these people. But then . . .

"I know him." My surprise forced its way out.

"I'm sorry?" her voice said behind me.

I studied the poster more closely. "Well, I don't know him personally. But this guy, he was at the museum yesterday."

"What's that now?" That voice was lower, entirely masculine. I spun to see a man in a khaki uniform shirt with an actual star-shaped badge. He was probably thirty-five or forty, with thick dark hair and a mustache. My whole body went hot. No, not because he was good-looking, although I suppose he was. I could recognize that without getting worked up over it. But I'd been talking to the sheriff for all of five seconds and already gone off script.

"Hi," I squeaked. "I work at the Banditt Museum. I just started this week. I'm replacing Reggie Heap."

He studied me as if memorizing my features so he could put out an APB. "Are you now? Well, welcome to town."

"Thanks. Er, this is kind of weird, and I don't know if you can do anything about it, but I thought I should tell you."

"About that man?" He gestured toward the WANTED posters.

"No. Well, yes, but that's not why I came. I didn't know he was wanted. But I saw him in the museum yesterday. He was hanging around the gems and minerals room for about half an hour. That's really all I can tell you. I didn't speak to him. As far as I know he didn't do anything illegal there." Did I sound like I was defending him or downplaying the sighting? I was instinctively distancing myself from the wanted stranger—nothing to do with me!—when I should try to get the sheriff to investigate.

He stood beside me facing the board. "Which fellow was it?"

I pointed to the poster, which had his name, FAUSTO YUBETA, WANTED IN CONNECTION WITH SEVERAL VIOLENT CRIMES, 5'1", 100 POUNDS, 28 YEARS OLD. Not a lot of information, and maybe the description didn't sound physically threatening, but *violent crimes* chilled me. Had a violent criminal actually been in the museum, a few dozen feet away from me, with no one else around?

Violent as in hitting someone on the head with a rock? A criminal actually returning to the scene of the crime?

"Interesting." The sheriff looked at me, his dark eyes seeming to peer into my mind. "How sure are you? You saw someone at the museum, but you didn't speak to him . . . Most people would probably just notice a Hispanic man. There are plenty of those around here."

Okay, he was really asking if I was racist enough to see a skinny Hispanic man and assume he must be the criminal on the poster. But I'm fairly good with faces, and I'd observed him for half an hour, on and off, when I'd been nervous and paying more attention than I might normally.

I couldn't explain that last part. Also, could I be one hundred percent sure?

"Well, I could be wrong," I admitted. "But the guy at the museum definitely looked like this. Skinny, same face shape, maybe a few years older but this could be an older photo. His hair was a bit longer and he had a thin mustache, I think."

"You're not sure if he had a mustache?"

None of this conversation was causing the heat to recede from my face. I probably looked like I'd eaten way too many hot peppers.

"Look, obviously *you* have a mustache," I said. "His was more like little wispy hairs on his upper lip. I wasn't close enough to decide whether that was a mustache or he just hadn't shaved in a while and can't grow a real beard."

"How far away were you?"

"Twenty to thirty feet, I guess. But he was there for a while." I had a feeling the sheriff was going to dismiss my claims of seeing the guy at the museum. I couldn't entirely blame him.

He nodded, frowning. "If you see him again, give us a call. I doubt he'll be back though."

That was probably true, and a gentle way to dismiss my concerns. I nodded, avoiding his gaze and wishing I'd stayed at the museum despite the potential murderer.

"Anyway, I'm Victor Johnson." He held out his hand.

"Petra Cloch." I hoped my hand wasn't noticeably sweaty as we shook.

"Newest member of the Banditt staff, huh?"

"Yep." I tried to smile. "I've been in town two days and I'm already finding creative ways to humiliate myself."

A burst of laughter came from the girl behind the desk, loud enough to make me jump a little.

"That's Elena," Victor said. "Our ray of sunshine. But you had something else to report." He waved me toward his office. "Come in and tell me about it."

# Chapter Ten

THE SHERIFF TOOK me down the hall to an office that was almost as big as the front room. It had two large wooden desks forming an L, with bookcases along the wall behind them. Victor went around the desks to sit, waving me to one of the two chairs across from him. The chair's hard leather squeaked under me as I sat.

Victor leaned his elbows on the desk, his hands folded together. "So, how can I help you?"

"I'm not sure . . . It might be nothing you can do anything about." I took a deep breath as I pulled out the laptop. "As you know, Reggie Heap died recently."

He nodded. "A tragic accident."

"Was it an accident?" I hadn't intended to ask that, but it had been on my mind and popped out of my mouth.

"Well, I guess it was a heart attack that caused the car accident. Tragic either way."

Whew, he'd thought I was saying a heart attack wasn't an accident. That kind of made me look like a jerk, but I didn't have to explain why I thought Reggie's death wasn't an accident at all.

I could move on . . . but it wouldn't seem too strange that Reggie's replacement was curious about his death, would it? Morbid things fascinated plenty of people, and I had a connection to Reggie, even if I'd never met him.

"How did you decide the heart attack killed him? If his car ran off the mountain road, I'm surprised anyone knew he'd had a heart attack first." I opened my eyes wide, trying to look innocent. Let the sheriff think I was naïve or even dumb as long as he didn't realize what I really was.

"That would be a question for the medical examiner," Victor said. "I suppose it doesn't really matter—either way, he's dead—but officially the cause of death was a heart attack."

Shoot, I had no excuse to ask the medical examiner questions.

I barreled ahead with the awkwardness. "The news said you found him."

"Some people who'd been up hiking called in about a car off the road. I drove out to check, so I was the first officer on the scene." Victor smiled but his eyebrows drew together. "Is this about Reggie's death? There wasn't anything suspicious about it."

*That's what you think.*

But I couldn't go there. "It's about Reggie. I know he's dead, but . . . Well, I've moved into his job, and his house. Apparently he didn't have any close relatives or friends, so I'm finding a lot of his personal belongings. Including this."

I set the laptop on the desk, opened it, and typed in the password. I brought up a file folder and spun the laptop so Victor could see the screen. He stared at it for a few seconds. Then his gaze shifted to study me.

I cleared my throat. "I was thinking about deleting all his files so I could use the laptop, if no one else claimed it. But then I saw what kind of files he had."

Victor frowned and tapped at the laptop. He frowned some more. I forced myself to sit back and wait quietly.

Finally he said, "Okay, I see how upsetting this must have been. I admit, I wouldn't have expected it of Reggie."

"Oh. You knew him?" I don't know why that surprised me. In a town this size, most people probably knew each other. That was an uncomfortable thought.

"Not well, but enough to recognize on the street. He was pretty quiet, kept to himself." Victor blew out a breath. "Come to think of it, exactly the kind of guy who does something crazy and the neighbors all say, *I never would have guessed. He was so quiet and polite.*"

"Yeah." I don't know why I said that. "I never met him, but I'm starting to get a picture."

"I don't want to dismiss your concerns," Victor said, "but viewing porn isn't illegal. I don't see any evidence that Reggie was *making* porn. Not that that's necessarily illegal either."

"Well, yeah, but teen girls? I'm not sure what age would count as child pornography . . . And obviously, you can't do anything about Reggie, but I felt like I ought to say something."

"I'm glad to know our newest citizen is so conscientious." Was he teasing me? I couldn't read him well enough to say. He went on. "The thing is, these videos might be years old, and they probably weren't taken in New Mexico. And those girls could have been over eighteen but made to look younger. Think about all the TV shows that have high school students played by people in their twenties. It can be hard to tell."

I nodded. "So there's nothing anyone can do."

"I'll tell you what. Leave the computer with me. I'll note the sites where he got these videos and send them to the FBI. They may already know about them, but if not . . . Then I can wipe the computer and give it back to you, assuming there's no evidence of anything criminal that we need to keep."

"You'll check though?"

"You have my word. I appreciate that you brought this to me."

Some of the tension seeped out of my shoulders. This was the most I could hope to achieve. Maybe Victor would actually look at Reggie's email in more detail, or assign someone to do it, or the FBI would. They'd certainly have a better chance of spotting something suspicious than I would. And if they found evidence that he'd been involved in something that got him killed, I wouldn't have to explain my suspicions.

"Thanks," I said. "I don't need the computer back." As much as I would like a free laptop, that one had bad associations now.

"Just as well, as these things can take months. Is there anything else?"

"Oh, you'll need the password. I'll write it down for you."

He slid a notepad over and I carefully wrote out *SchistHappens*, making sure all the letters were clear. I gave back the pad.

He looked at what I'd written. "How did you get his password?"

I shifted and the chair squeaked. "He left a note." Technically, that wasn't *completely* false, if you squinted from a distance.

Victor sighed and shook his head. "Well, I guess that was good in this case." He pushed his chair back, ready to rise.

It was tempting to flee, but I took a moment to think. I'd handed over the laptop and reported the suspicious man at the museum. The sheriff had seemed to take me seriously—although as an elected official, maybe he was good at pretending to take people seriously when they came in with crackpot theories.

"I don't know quite how to put this," I finally said. "I found this on Reggie's laptop, and his keys are missing, and now seeing the WANTED poster with the guy who was at the museum yesterday . . . I don't know. It just feels like something strange is happening. But then, I'm new in town, so everything seems a bit strange."

Victor chuckled. "I expect so, especially if you're working at the Banditt Museum."

"Yeah, it's . . . different."

We smiled in agreement.

"I'm working in Reggie's office and living in his house," I explained. "I just want to make absolutely certain nothing is, well, wrong."

He studied me for several seconds. I tried not to look like a nut job. I don't know how successful I was.

Finally he said, "I hope you won't take this the wrong way, but frankly, if something is wrong, you should stay out of it." He plucked a card from a holder on the desk and slid it across to me. "Feel free to call me if you're worried. Definitely call if you see that guy back at the museum, but you can call if anything makes you uneasy. Please don't go looking for trouble though. I expect Reggie was just a lonely guy who turned to online pornography because it was easier than dealing with real people, but if he was mixed up in something, stay away from it."

I hadn't been looking for trouble when I picked up the fluorite crystals. Maybe I had been looking since then—although I'd never imagined seeing someone I recognized on a WANTED poster. But Victor seemed convinced that Reggie's death had been natural, and I couldn't explain why

I thought otherwise. Possibly I was wrong. Not about the memories I'd gotten from the crystal, but about Reggie being involved. But if not Reggie, then whom?

Maybe I could come up with some excuse for why I'd been looking at the fluorite crystals closely, through a magnifying lens, and found blood, if I looked and did find it.

But for the moment, I could only nod. "Thanks for your time."

He stood and offered his hand again, with a smile that could go on his reelection posters. "That's what I'm here for. I'll walk you out."

"No need. I've taken up enough of your time." I grabbed my mostly empty backpack and fled.

The hallway had three more doors off of it, presumably other offices, a records room, maybe a lab, although maybe no lab in a town this size. I turned toward the front room and stepped through that door.

The young woman—Elena, Victor had called her—smiled at me. "Was the sheriff able to help you?"

"He was very kind." Helpful was another question, but he'd seemed to take me seriously.

"Sorry, I don't mean to be nosy. Wait, that's a lie." Her nose wrinkled. It was kind of adorable. "I love being nosy. But I didn't mean to pry into your personal business."

"It's okay." What else could I say?

"I overheard you telling the sheriff you work at the museum now. I guess that means you rent from Miss Shelley."

"Yes. You call her *Miss* Shelley?" Was I supposed to call her that? I was used to the informality of the Seattle area, but TV shows suggested Southern states were more formal. I hadn't thought of New Mexico as *Southern*, but it was pretty far south.

"She was my kindergarten teacher. Of course, that's more than twenty years ago now. I just wish she was still teaching so my kids could have her."

"Your kids . . . Wait, you were in kindergarten over twenty years ago? How old *are* you?"

Her laughter burst out, so loud and shrill I winced. "I'm twenty-eight. My kids are eight, six, three, and seven months. My husband is one of the deputies here."

"Wow. You don't look like a mother of four. Or I guess you do, since you are, but . . . You know what I mean." At least I hoped she did, because I was digging myself into a deeper hole as I tried to recover from my shock.

"No offense taken." She looked smug.

Movement caught my eye through the glass panel in the door that led to the offices. Someone had approached the door, I thought, but they'd retreated again. Someone who didn't want to interrupt? Someone trying to avoid Elena's loud laughter? Sheriff Victor, wanting to leave the building but not wanting to deal with me any longer?

I was probably getting paranoid.

"Did you really see one of them?" Elena gestured toward

the WANTED posters.

"I think so." I turned toward the board. "Maybe." I was fairly certain, so why was I being so wishy-washy? Was I really more afraid of being wrong and looking foolish than I was of a violent criminal in my workplace? Apparently.

Elena came around the desk and stood next to me. "Which one?"

I pointed.

She studied the poster. "That's so wild! I can't believe you saw a wanted criminal your first week here."

That surprised a laugh out of me. "You must've seen plenty of criminals." I gestured toward the jail cells.

"Oh, we don't use those. They're historical. Sometimes tourists come in and take pictures of themselves in there. It's listed on the town tourism map. Actual criminals go to the police station."

"Probably safer. So you don't see criminals at all?" I resisted adding, *And you* want *to?*

She looked at me, eyes dancing. "We don't actually get that many. Some drunk driving, an occasional fight." Her lips turned down. "Some domestic abuse. That's the worst, unless a drunk driver kills someone, but—anyway, not so many *real* criminals. I mean, the others are guilty of crimes, but it's not their job title. I've been putting up these posters for years and I've never seen anyone who was on one."

"Right. I guess that makes sense in a town this size." My mind raced. So what about Reggie? Had his death been one of those impulsive, almost accidental things? A fight with a drunken friend? I'd sensed shock at what the killer had done but also a sense of startled pride. That might suggest someone who didn't have experience with violence but had a lot of buried anger that burst out.

But surely in that case the killer would have simply fled the scene. Instead, they were sober and clever enough to stage the car accident.

And was it simply a coincidence that a known criminal showed up two weeks later? In a town of 2000 people, where even someone working in the sheriff's office rarely saw a *real criminal*, that seemed unlikely.

"Are you okay?" Elena asked.

"What?" I'd been staring at the WANTED poster. "I'm fine. Just . . . wondering."

She nodded. "It must be scary, but I doubt he'll come back. He's probably in Mexico by now."

My thoughts elsewhere, I mumbled, "Oh?"

"We're only a few hours from the border. I'm not saying criminals pour over the border from Mexico or anything. I'm not one of those people who think we need to build a wall to keep out the evil foreigners." She lowered her voice. "Though you will meet people like that around here. And I hate to say it, but Hispanic people whose families have been here for generations can be the snobbiest about new immigrants. My family . . ." She rolled her eyes and shook her head.

"Got it. Then why . . ."

"Why do I think he went to Mexico? If a criminal wanted to escape, that's probably where they'd go, right? Head to El Paso, cross the border to Juárez, disappear."

"You'd know better than I would. I came from Washington state, closer to the Canada border. Wouldn't it be hard to get past border control?"

"It's easier to go south than come back north. He could probably just take a bus across if he had ID from Mexico, or a good fake ID."

"Huh." The real question was, *had* Fausto Yubeta wanted to escape? Surely someone who was trying to flee the country wouldn't wander through a museum first. He had to be there for a reason.

Assuming it was the same person. The world population was over, what, eight billion now? Lots of people looked similar. But if I started questioning everything I saw, I wouldn't get anywhere. So I'd assume the man I saw in the museum was this wanted criminal. In that case, surely it was safe to assume he was there for a reason, and the reason wasn't interest in rocks and minerals. But what was it?

He'd spent half an hour in the rocks and minerals room. Had he touched anything, maybe leaned his hand on a display case? If so, had it been enough to leave impressions behind? Few people came back there, and probably most didn't touch the cases. Maybe that guy hadn't either. Even if he didn't expect anyone to check for fingerprints on the glass, it might be second nature for a criminal to avoid leaving them.

I didn't relish the thought of checking all the cases in the area where I'd seen the man, hoping I'd find something. Then I'd have to figure out if the impressions came from him, and what they meant.

I could leave it all to Sheriff Victor now. But he only knew about Reggie's porn habit. Once he reported that to the FBI, Victor wasn't likely to pursue it further. He might also assume Fausto Yubeta was long gone, if he even believed I'd seen the man.

So much for avoiding further investigation.

# Chapter Eleven

I'D USED UP too much of my lunch hour to go home, so I stopped at a food truck with a sign that said BURRITO SHACK and ate at a picnic table in a tiny park. Then I headed back to the museum, thinking about what I knew and what I could learn.

I knew Reggie watched porn with teen girls. (Okay, technically I only knew he had it on his computer, but it seemed a safe bet that he actually watched it.) Did he keep his interest online, or could he have pestered someone in person? If so, who? Haven was the youngest employee at the museum. She wasn't a teen. Was she close enough for Reggie's taste?

Come to think of it, she'd said some odd things about Reggie. She clearly didn't like him. I'd thought she'd been criticizing his work ethic, but when Liberty said Reggie was harmless, Haven said, *He is now, anyway.* We'd all treated it as an awkward bit of morbid humor, but maybe she'd meant it, that he hadn't been so harmless before.

It was hard to imagine her killing Reggie though. Maybe in self-defense if he'd attacked her. Yeah, I could believe she'd fight back hard. But the rest of it—somehow getting his body to his car, driving out to the mountain, and staging an accident—I didn't see it. If she'd been acting in self-defense, why not say so? It would be unpleasant, but less risky than getting caught hauling a dead body around.

So I'd talk to Haven, but maybe Reggie had contact with other teen girls, despite his reputation as a loner.

Gloria was behind the counter when I entered the museum. After we exchanged greetings, I asked, "Are there other employees I haven't met yet? Maybe other teens who come in after school, like Austin?"

"Yes, Austin alternates with a girl called Ingrid."

"Do the teens only work here at the counter, or do they help out in the exhibit rooms too?"

"In the summer, we have docents who wander through the museum keeping an eye on things and answering questions. We tried teenagers, but they just wanted to hang out together." She glanced toward the gift shop where three teen girls were giggling. "Now we use retired people and women who want a few hours of work while the kids are at a summer program. That's worked out better."

"Makes sense. When did you switch from using teens?" I hoped people would answer if I acted like my questions were perfectly ordinary and I stopped before anyone got so suspicious or weirded out they grabbed the torches and pitchforks.

"Oh, it must be four or five years ago now," Gloria said.

Before Reggie came to the museum. Gloria was looking a little puzzled, but this was important, so I plowed on. "Do you ever have young interns?"

Her eyebrows drew together. "We haven't had interns, but I suppose it's a possibility. Do you want one?"

I shrugged. "It wouldn't hurt to have help when I install items from the new donation."

"Kit could help you with that, and Austin if things are slow up here."

"Okay, thanks. Oh, is there a digital catalog of the museum's artifacts?"

"I'm afraid we never got around to that, what with all the early artifacts already on paper. But if you want to digitize your records, feel free."

"Right." I couldn't think of any other questions, or at least any she could answer that wouldn't make me look as peculiar as I am. I said goodbye and headed back toward the rocks and minerals wing.

What had I learned? Ingrid normally worked up front, but Reggie might have asked her back to his area to help with something. Locked the geology room door so no one could disturb them as he hit on her.

If it turned out Haven or Ingrid had killed Reggie because he tried to assault one of them, I'd have a hard time proving it. Plus I could sympathize with fighting back. But self-defense was one thing. If they'd come forward at the time, it would have been manslaughter, if that. Covering up the killing was another matter. Maybe they'd panicked and staging Reggie's death seemed logical. But didn't they say people who murdered successfully could get a taste for it and see it as a way to solve other problems?

But Reggie getting killed when he tried to assault Haven or Ingrid wouldn't explain Fausto Yubeta. What if he was involved in human trafficking and brought a girl to Reggie? And she'd fought back and fled . . . But that didn't explain why she'd tried to make it look like an accident, or why Fausto Yubeta returned to the museum two weeks later. Maybe he'd sold a girl to Reggie, and now Fausto was looking for the girl. If so, I hoped she escaped.

Maybe I could find an article about Yubeta, see what specifically he was wanted for. I pulled out my phone with a sigh. I didn't want to use Reggie's laptop now that I knew what he had on it, and what he probably did while he used it, but I was still disappointed not to have a free computer to take home. Maybe Haven could find a donated machine that wasn't needed for display. I could ask Peyton if the museum would supply one for the office. It was a little odd that Reggie hadn't had one, but the files were all on paper and it sounded like he didn't do much anyway, so maybe he hadn't wanted one.

A search for Fausto Yubeta didn't turn up anything except the same wanted announcement. *Violent crimes* didn't tell me much. I guess it left out cybercrimes, fraud, and probably pickpocketing. But it left in everything from robbery to murder.

I wandered back toward Haven's area. At least that's what I intended. Somehow I wound up in a long room full of classic cars and old wagons. The black, horse-drawn hearse was particularly interesting. The sides were carved to look like draped curtains and it had a small coffin inside—presumably empty. I wasn't quite to the point where I'd assume the museum had a mummified body in there. Maybe tomorrow.

I also paused at a stagecoach-type wagon with huge wheels, chests of drawers inside, and an arched canvas top. Thinking about crossing the country in one of those put my problems in perspective. Kit was right—I ought to learn the museum thoroughly, so if lost tourists wandered into my area, I could point them in the right direction. Not that heading in the right direction would necessarily get you to your destination.

Haven did the more modern stuff, so I kept going until I found myself on Route 66. Songs from the fifties played from hidden speakers. The room had neon motel signs, an old gas pump, and a classic Corvette that was wider than the doors. Did they take it apart and move it in pieces, or had the room been built around it?

It took me a minute to notice Haven tacking up a sign. Her dress, either vintage or a retro copy, was a deep red with a flared skirt to midcalf. Panels of black with white polka-dot fabric were inset in the skirt. I joined her.

She glanced at me. "Hey."

"New exhibit?"

"Yeah. I want to go beyond the glamour side of Route 66. I did an exhibit of offensive Native American tourist trinkets." She pointed to the left. "I'm finally getting to this display on sundown towns."

"On what now?"

"Places where African Americans weren't allowed to be after dark. It took a while to collect enough material."

I studied the signs on the wall, which said things like WHITES ONLY. I pointed to one that said, THIS IS KU KLUX KLAN COUNTRY and asked, "They advertised that?"

She raised a penciled eyebrow cynically. "They were proud of it."

"Right. Wow."

She put her hammer into a toolbox. "Telling the truth about the era wasn't Peyton's priority, but I wore him down. Next up, the Japanese internment camps, even if I have to take down some of the old license plates."

"So you're not just into the Route 66 styles."

"Yeah, I can love some things about the era and hate others. Have you been to the diner in the old train car? *Fabulous* chicken fried steak. And the malts." She gave a dreamy sigh, as if she was talking about a love interest instead of food. Or maybe food was her love interest. "The décor is really fun too. Anyway, did you want something, or are you lost?" She grinned. "Or both? Around here, it's usually both."

"Right." I gave myself a mental shake to get back on

track. "So I have a weird question, but I hope you won't mind. Was Reggie . . . Well, a creep?"

Her crimson lips twisted in disgust. "You could say that. At least, *I* could say that. I'm not sure how *you* know."

"I found evidence that he was, um, interested in fairly young women."

Haven snorted. "That's a delicate way of putting it. He didn't *do* anything, but he liked to hang around in here sometimes. Especially when I was wearing a skirt. I finally told him to knock it off."

"Did you complain to the Banditts?"

"Nah, like I said, he didn't actually do or say anything inappropriate. He just looked."

"If it made you uncomfortable, it was inappropriate."

"Okay, point. But I didn't need to run to Mom and Dad over it. I can take care of myself." One eyebrow rose, emphasizing the dark arch. It was oddly fascinating, like her whole face was more expressive with the dramatic makeup. "Still not sure why you care," she added.

"I hope he didn't bother visitors. Or the girl that works upfront sometimes, Ingrid."

Haven grinned. She had a smudge of lipstick on her front teeth. "I guess you haven't met Ingrid. She's a sturdy farm girl with a brown belt in aikido. She could smack down Reggie no problem."

I blinked. "There's an aikido studio in town?"

"I know, right? You can't necessarily find everything you want here, but we have some delightfully unexpected things."

Did that make it more or less likely that Reggie had hit on Ingrid and she'd fought back? If she knew aikido, why grab a heavy object for defense? But maybe she'd never used martial arts in a real fight and forgot her training in a panic. Meanwhile, Haven had a reason to dislike Reggie, but not a reason to kill him—assuming she was telling the truth, and assuming she didn't have an entirely unrelated reason.

"Does it matter?" Haven asked. "Reggie's dead. Maybe I ought to feel worse about that, but . . ." She shrugged.

"I don't know," I said. "It's just weird moving into his office and his house. I feel like I know him even though I've never met him and won't now. I guess I'm wondering what he's done that might come back to haunt me."

"Well, you don't strike me as the type to sexually harass anyone. The opposite, I'd say."

What did that mean? She wasn't wrong, and it wasn't an insult, but still. I didn't want to probe that any further though.

"Thanks for telling me," I said. "I'd like to hear more about the real Route 66 era sometime, if you're not sick of talking about it."

"Never. Hey, I don't suppose you swing dance." She took a step back from the display and spun. Her red skirt flared out, a mesmerizing blur, and then settled down over her hips again.

"Never tried it," I said. "I'm not much of a dancer."

"Too bad. Not that this is a huge swing dancing community. More like country line dancing, but at least that's similar in some ways."

"I'll have to take your word for it." And I needed to escape before I got roped into trying line dancing. "Anyway, I'd better get back to work."

"Stop by anytime."

"Thanks. Um, you have lipstick on your teeth."

She heaved a sigh. "I usually do. Thanks. I'll fix it." She turned with a wave and strode away with her skirt swishing. She'd probably check her lipstick in one of those compacts with a mirror in the flip-up lid.

I went the other way, hoping it would lead me to the geology wing. It did, eventually. The display room was empty of visitors. I ought to work on changing that if I wanted to keep this job.

I unlocked my office door and dropped my backpack in the corner. I'd forgotten to ask Haven if she had any extra computers. Well, it wasn't hard to find her. Or rather, it *was* hard to find her, but only because of the confusing museum layout. I'd run into her again soon even if I didn't go looking.

I stood for a moment, debating what to do next. Then I noticed something on the desk that hadn't been there when I left.

A ring of several dozen tiny keys.

# Chapter Twelve

MAYBE PEYTON HAD found the case keys and left them in my office. But Gloria hadn't said anything . . . Or had a killer stolen the keys, used them, and returned them—using a copy of my office door key?

My legs went numb and my head throbbed. I sank into the office chair, rested my elbows on the desk—not near the keys—and pressed my knuckles against my eyes. Fine. I had the keys now. And I knew not to leave anything valuable in the office, or anything that would arouse suspicions of my suspicions that Reggie had been murdered.

I dropped my hands and glared at the keys. I could put on gloves before using them, but I ought to figure out if they had anything to tell me.

Sometimes I hate my life.

Didn't I have anything else I could pretend was a higher priority? I checked the moving company's delivery schedule for my shipping container. But that took less than five minutes, and nothing would be there until the next day, at the earliest, so I didn't have an excuse to flee the museum early.

I needed to sort the new donation and plan new displays. That would take weeks, and I wouldn't feel safe settling into museum curator mode until I knew I wasn't stuck in the middle of whatever had gotten Reggie killed.

At least my headache had receded as I pondered how to avoid the problem. It probably wouldn't stay gone for long, of course. I suspected I had a lot of headaches in my near future, what with the shocking mess Reggie had left behind. To be clear, I'm talking about his chaotic filing system, although the suspicious death was also a shocking mess.

I checked again that the big room was empty. One of these days, I was going to get so used to being alone back here that I'd forget to check. Then I'd probably look up from doing something embarrassing and find an entire busload of tourists watching me.

But not today, so no more excuses. I breathed deeply and set my hand on the keys.

*What? No! Where is it?*

Anger, frustration. Hope turned to rage.

I flinched back, took another breath, and pressed harder, trying to see past that one moment.

Excitement. Greed. *It's mine now.*

Behind that, a vague sense of annoyance. Apathy. The keys were too much trouble. And a brief spark of someone happy, not the greedy excitement but just that the keys were a path to something else.

I sat back and tried to sort it all out. Psychometry doesn't give me a complete history of everything that happened, in chronological order. If someone had frequently worn or held an object and often had the same emotion, that would leave a mark, even if the emotion wasn't that dramatic. It was like a stream wearing a path into rock through repetition. A single episode of a less powerful emotion might only hang around for days, or just a few hours. But an intense emotion might leave residue for a century, even if it had only happened once, like a flash flood blasting down a streambed and tumbling boulders into new positions.

So I had to note the strength of everything left behind and use that to guess what had happened when. I thought the vague annoyance was from Reggie. He hadn't kept the keys on him, so he hadn't left a lot of emotion behind (fortunately, as I'd had more than enough of him). From what I'd seen, he wasn't particularly organized or tidy. He probably had to look for the keys whenever he needed them, and the repetition of annoyance had settled in like the patina that builds up on copper. (Yes, I'm mixing my metaphors now, but they're all geology based, so that's something.)

The first emotion I felt was probably the last one laid down. It could be the same person who'd been excited about having the keys, believing he or she was about to get what they wanted. But they'd been disappointed—frustrated and angry.

So. I'd picked up yet more jumbled impressions that didn't actually tell me much useful. If you've been thinking I have a responsibility to use my *gift* to help people, now you know why I don't feel that way. As far as gifts go, it was worse than getting a pair of socks. In fact, I can totally appreciate a cozy, warm pair of socks, or something fun, like the ones I have with the geologic timescale. Psychometry was more like a gift of perfume I was allergic to. It made me feel lousy and it didn't do much for anyone else.

At least there was one good thing about finding the keys: I had the keys. Now I could start matching them to the various cases. While I was at it, I could check more closely for anything missing, and look for emotional residue from Fausto Yubeta or anyone else who might be involved in . . . whatever.

How fun.

The rocks and minerals room was about fifty feet long and thirty feet wide. Six display cases with shelves sat along one of the long walls, each about six feet wide. Locked glass doors meant visitors could look but not touch. Those shelves had smaller samples, items that would be easy to slip into a pocket. The other long wall held open shelves with big rocks and minerals. Nothing prevented visitors from touching them beyond the expectation that you weren't supposed to touch things in museums. But they were big and heavy, so they'd be hard to steal.

The middle of the room had pedestals with the biggest rock samples, like a thirty-inch-high amethyst geode that looked like a gaping mouth full of deep purple crystal teeth.

That was worth a few thousand dollars but also probably weighed over a hundred pounds. I tried to rock it and it didn't budge, so it was affixed to the base somehow for extra security. The middle of the room also held cases that were about two feet by two feet with glass tops, also locked.

The keys were actually labeled with numbers, which was a pleasant surprise. However, someone had simply written the numbers on the keys in marker, so half of them were hard to read, either because the number had partly rubbed off or because the cramped, poor handwriting made it difficult to tell a one from a seven and three from an eight. After hunting around, I found numbers on the cases, but they were tiny and in awkward places. Also the numbering system seemed completely random, not matching the layout of cases. Nothing about this museum was tidy. Add to the task list: Set up a new number system and label the keys appropriately.

Oh, right, looking for clues—I didn't find any. Nothing missing, as far as I could tell without finding all the records and comparing them to the items on display. Even then, if I found discrepancies I'd give it a seventy percent chance of being due to incompetence rather than theft. I found plenty of fingerprints and dust, but most seemed to be from child-sized hands. The fingerprints, that is. The dust presumably came from the desert and was everywhere, although the closed glass cases protected the samples better than the open shelves did. Not that the dust would hurt the samples, but it dulled the shine on all the pretty minerals.

I didn't pick up anything useful through psychometry. It had been a long shot.

On the bright side, I got pretty familiar with what was in all the cases, and my task list was growing longer. Wait, only the first part of that was a bright side. I didn't mind having a long list of tasks, since I'd be employed forever if Peyton was willing to pay me until I'd finished. But it was still annoying to know I had so much to do because the prior person in the position had been lazy and sloppy.

I'm not saying Reggie deserved to die. I will admit to some satisfaction that he was gone though. And if there was an afterlife, I hoped he would spend his endlessly cleaning rock samples. (If you don't know how tedious and unpleasant that is, substitute *toilets* for *rock samples* and you'll have the idea.)

I'd gone through the whole room, growing increasingly cranky. A few tourists came in. At first I tried greeting them with a friendly (I hoped) "Hi, come on in! I'm just doing inventory." But that seemed to make people uncomfortable. They glanced around awkwardly and left within a couple of minutes. When I tried ignoring people, a few visitors actually went through the room. I guess I wasn't the only one who felt more comfortable if no one paid attention to me. Or else my greeting wasn't as friendly as I thought. Or maybe by late afternoon I was so covered in dust I blended in and no one noticed me.

I ended up in a corner of the room that had displays related to mining. The nearest glass-fronted shelves held things like a nineteenth-century miner's headlamp and a scale with brass weights, alongside samples of the minerals that had been mined in this region—bright green malachite and deep blue azurite, manganese oxide with its fuzzy crystals like black velvet (I'd had to check the label for the name of that one), twisty blobs of copper, and some calcite nuggets with bright flecks of gold.

An extremely rusty old mining cart sat in the corner, its wheels perched on a section of railway track. It was about four feet long, at least two feet wide, and over three feet high. The cart had a couple of candy wrappers in it. To get those out, I'd have to lean way over and hope I could reach. Or find a stepstool or tongs, but that sounded like too much work at the moment. I stood on my toes, leaned my rib cage on the edge of the cart, and reached down.

The cart moved. Not a lot, but it definitely shifted an inch, while I yelped and scrambled for balance.

I stepped back and glared at the cart. I'd assumed it was welded to the rails. So much for shortcuts—or assuming anything sensible. That was a safety hazard and had to be fixed. Granted, most people wouldn't touch the cart—though that might fall into the category of an assumption I shouldn't make—and it was too heavy to go flying across the room at a touch, but it was still clearly unsafe, if only to me.

I gave up on retrieving the candy wrappers and crawled

around looking for any kind of ID number.

"There you are," a cheerful voice boomed.

I jerked my head up and smacked it against the metal. The thud sounded like I'd hit the mine cart with a mallet. I sat back, blinking away stars.

Sheriff Victor came around the mining cart. "Sorry. I didn't mean to startle you." He held out his hand to help me up.

"It's okay." I pretended not to see his hand. I twisted to kneel and then grabbed the edge of an old cast iron safe, over two feet high. With one hand still braced on the safe, I rubbed the top of my head. It was tender but I wouldn't follow in Reggie's steps with a fatal head injury—yet, anyway.

The sheriff frowned at my hand on the safe. Was he shocked because I was touching a museum exhibit? It wasn't like I could hurt the safe. More likely I'd leave a cleaner space in the dust. But touching museum exhibits was generally prohibited. Maybe the sheriff was debating arresting me. Laughter bubbled up in my chest at the idea.

I cleared my throat. "I guess I was so focused I didn't realize anyone had come in the room."

He shifted his gaze to the mining cart. "What had you so fascinated?"

"More like frustrated." I edged around the car so I wasn't trapped in the corner. Not that Victor had given me any reason to fear him, but my heart was still racing. Also, experience has taught me to be overcautious. Not, like, negative experience with men specifically. Just with people who could turn on you if they decided you were a freak.

"The records for this room are a mess," I explained. "I was looking for any kind of ID number on the mining cart."

He nodded, glancing around. "I guess you've got your work cut out for you here." His gaze settled on the old safe. "I wonder where Peyton picked up that thing. It must weigh a ton."

"A few hundred pounds anyway. I don't know how he got half the stuff moved into the museum. Heavy equipment? A lot of muscle and determination?"

"Probably the latter. Peyton is a force to be reckoned with. Knowing him, it came stocked with gold nuggets."

The safe had a brass dial in the closed door. A combination lock, so no need for my keys. I grabbed the handle but it didn't budge. "I wonder when it was last opened. Maybe not since it's been in the museum. I suppose it's closed so there's no risk a child would crawl inside and get locked in."

"There's a gruesome thought. You're probably right though. I doubt there's anything in it." Victor grinned. "Unless Peyton got it this way and it hasn't been open for generations. Who knows, there could be treasure inside!"

"Right. You never know." Except I highly doubted anyone had left valuables in the safe for so long.

On the other hand . . . Stranger things had already happened that week.

# Chapter Thirteen

"IF I CAN find a record of the safe, it could list the combination," I said.

"Yeah? It would be fun to see it opened." He glanced toward the office. "*If* you can find a record? Is there some doubt?"

"Oh, you have no idea. I've just glanced through the records, but at best, someone wasn't very good at alphabetizing, and at worst, no one cared."

He winced sympathetically. "Ouch."

Victor had yet to explain why he was here, but my throat was parched and I wanted to sit, so I headed to the office. "Come on in, if you want." That's me being friendly and welcoming.

Inside, I dropped the keys on my desk and grabbed my water bottle. I drank deeply, washing the dust out of my mouth and parched throat. "Sorry, I'd offer you something to drink but I'm not yet set up for guests."

"No problem." He sat in the second chair and stretched out his long legs, looking around. Apparently he intended to stay a while. He twisted to see the shelves of minerals. "Cool rocks. Yours, or were they here?"

I went hot and cold and tingly. "They were here," I croaked.

I'd left the fluorite crystals on the shelf where Peyton had put them, since I couldn't figure out what else to do with them. I suddenly realized I'd invited the sheriff into a crime scene. Would he notice something I'd missed? Be able to spot bloodstains in the mottled carpet? That could solve my problem . . .

But he turned back and studied the poster on the wall behind me. Clearly *he* didn't have psychic powers.

I checked the time on my phone: 5:38. "Wow, it's later than I realized. Did you need something from me? Or have something to tell me?" *Why are you here and will you please leave?*

"I dropped your keys off earlier."

"Oh, that was you?" I sagged with relief. "They were sitting on the desk when I got back after lunch."

He chuckled. "You thought maybe ghosts? After you left the office, I remembered I still had them. I held onto a few things pulled from the wreck until the investigation was formally closed."

"Investigation? I thought you were convinced it was an accident."

"I am. It was. But we still have to look at a sudden death."

Since he hadn't taken my hint, I sat too. "How do you

decide what is a police matter versus something for the sheriff's office?" Might as well fish for information.

"We work together a lot. The city hires the police, but the voters elect the sheriff. That way neither the police chief or the sheriff have too much power. Also, the police force generally focuses on the town. The sheriff's office handles the whole county." He looked proud of that. "But of course we ask the police for help if we need it. In the case of Mr. Heap's accident, we asked for an autopsy since it was an unexpected death. The autopsy showed he had a heart attack, and we found no signs that another vehicle was involved, so we assume the heart attack caused him to run off the road."

"His car must have been pretty mangled. Wasn't it hard to tell if another car had bumped it?"

"It was banged up, for sure, but we checked for traces of paint from another vehicle. Nothing."

"And a heart attack. Couldn't that be caused by some kind of poison or overdose of medicine?"

"Sure, and the coroner could check for that. I doubt he did in this case, since we had no reason to suspect anything." Victor's mustache hid his mouth, but I thought he was amused. "Why the interest?"

"No reason." I glanced past him at the fluorite crystals and then forced my gaze back to his. Did I look guilty? But I'd read that someone who meets your gaze for a long time without glancing away is probably lying, so maybe I should avoid looking at him too much.

I drank more water to give myself a moment to regroup. I put down the bottle and smiled. "Too many cop shows, probably. I've never actually met a sheriff before, so that was, um, new."

He grinned back. "I'd say we're the best law enforcement agents, but I might be biased."

Was he flirting? Did he think I'd been flirting? Why was he sticking around?

I cleared my throat. "Anyway, thanks for bringing the keys back. And answering my nosy questions. Um . . . I'll let you know if I find the combination to the safe, but don't hold your breath."

"I won't." He scanned the office as if cataloging everything in it. Maybe that was habit for someone in his job. Or was he looking for something? Maybe he had lied, and they were actually investigating Reggie's death as a homicide but keeping it secret. But if Victor had wanted to search Reggie's office, he could've found an excuse to do that before I got there.

I glanced at the ring of keys. "What did you do with the keys when you got here? This office was locked, and Gloria didn't say anything about the keys when I came in."

"I didn't see her. Kit said you weren't back from lunch yet so I gave him the keys."

I'd locked my office, so Kit must have a key to it. Or he'd borrowed the museum's set. I could hardly complain about a member of the owning family entering my office, since it was technically theirs, but it still felt like a breach of privacy. I'd have to remember that privacy wasn't part of this deal.

"So, you moved here from the Seattle area," Victor said. Apparently we were making small talk now. Lovely.

"That's right." Had I mentioned that at his office? I didn't think so. We hadn't talked about anything personal beyond the fact I worked at the museum.

"And you're a geologist."

I nodded. Other geologists might argue whether I actually deserve to be called a geologist with only a bachelor's degree in Earth Science, even with the geology emphasis. I'd never worked a job where my title was geologist, and I hadn't been accredited. I doubted Victor cared about those nuances.

"You know, New Mexico is one of the top states for oil and gas production," he said. "I'm surprised you didn't try to get work in that field."

I'd rather set myself up as a psychometry psychic than work for the petroleum industry, but I didn't need to tell Victor that. He sounded proud of the state's oil reserves, which no doubt brought in a lot of money and created jobs. But petroleum engineering degrees were losing favor, even for those who didn't care about the ethics. Young people understood that the world would have to switch away from gas eventually, possibly within the next twenty years. Who wanted a career in a field that would disappear soon?

"Not my area," I said. "I was happy enough to get this

job. I only got my bachelor's degree last year."

He nodded like he'd already known that. "You must have started late. Aren't you thirty?"

"I worked full-time and went to college part-time. Did you do a background check on me?"

"No, Kit told me."

"Kit talks too much," I grumbled.

Victor shook with silent laughter. "Small town, fast grapevine. You'll get used to it."

I grunted. "Did the gossips mention I have a lot of pets? I'd better get home to them." I started packing up my stuff. Nothing Victor knew was a secret, and I was probably the last person who had a right to complain about an invasion of privacy after the way I'd been snooping. Still. I actively avoided learning anything about people without their knowledge, most of the time. Reggie was an exception, but he was dead.

"Let me know when your stuff gets here and I'll help you unload," Victor said.

I stared at him. "I'm sure you have more important things to do."

His mustache twitched. "Nothing more important this week than welcoming the town's newest member."

I stared some more. He smiled back, seeming completely at ease. "Small town?" I asked.

He dipped his chin. "Small town."

"Right. Thanks." I didn't want to refuse his offer and

have him insist. Easier to simply not tell him when the pod got there. Although maybe he'd know before I did. I might have half the town showing up to help me unpack—and get a look at the new girl's stuff. I didn't come from a small town, but I knew generosity could be a cover for curiosity. I was probably the biggest excitement this town had had since, well, Reggie's car accident. And people didn't even know the half of it.

Victor rolled his neck, the way you do to get rid of kinks. "You haven't seen the guy from the WANTED poster again, right? You would have called me."

Oh, that could explain his visit. "I haven't."

"Nothing else odd or suspicious?"

I shook my head. That kept me from having to speak words that would be a lie. "It's been quiet here today—except for the ghost delivering keys."

He grinned. "Wouldn't that be nice? Helpful ghosts."

"Yeah, I could put them to work dusting. Hm, maybe they're staying away to avoid chores."

His eyes danced, and we shared a moment of amusement.

I couldn't have that. I checked the time again. Ten till six. Close enough. I put the key ring with all the case keys into my desk drawer and stood up. "Time to lock up." I grabbed my backpack.

Victor finally rose, but he waited at the office door for me. I locked that, and we walked through the big display room. I couldn't think of anything to say. Victor scanned the shelves. "I haven't been here in years. Not since I was a kid. I should visit again."

I didn't want to encourage him, but I couldn't discourage people from visiting the museum. I could only take my *weird hermit* thing so far when I basically had a hospitality job.

As I locked the door to the hallway, I settled on, "I'll be putting up new displays. Might be a while though."

"Oh, good. I can do a before-and after-tour." His eyes twinkled. "Maybe even check on your progress during."

Well, that had backfired. Victor seemed nice enough, but that didn't mean I wanted him hanging around. He was good-looking and probably charming to someone willing to be charmed. Plenty of people would love his company. It was a slow week (as far as he knew), and he wanted to know more about the new person in his community. Fair enough, but something would come along to distract him soon.

Or was every week a slow week in a town this size?

Well, if I could come up with evidence that Reggie was murdered, that would definitely give Sheriff Victor something else to think about.

I turned from the door. Victor waited, apparently planning to walk me out of the building. That would have been uncomfortable even if I was confident I could find my way out on the first try. I should have let him exit the room, locked the door behind him, and escaped the back way.

He shoved his hands in his front pockets. "Any interest in dinner? The diner's good."

I froze. I literally could not think of anything to say.

"Hey, Petra." Liberty walked down the hall toward us. "Victor." She nodded at him.

"Liberty," he muttered.

Liberty stopped a few feet away and looked at me. "You're coming to book club tonight, right?"

"Um." My mind was not working. Did I know anything about a book club?

"Don't tell me you forgot!" Liberty looked directly at me, basically shutting Victor out of the conversation. "You need to come tonight so you can weigh in on the next book we pick. Plus, drinks and nibbles!"

"You work fast," Victor said. I wasn't sure which of us he meant. "Is this Elena's book club?"

"Of course. You know her husband works tonight." To me, Liberty added, "Her mother takes the kids. Come on, I'll get you the address."

She turned and pulled Victor and me along in her wake. I still had no idea what was happening, but at least I'd dodged the dinner question.

At the next corner, Victor touched my arm to stop me as Liberty strode ahead. "You don't know Liberty very well yet," he whispered.

"I just met her yesterday." And now I was watching her stop halfway down the hall and turn back to look at us.

He nodded. "Just watch yourself around her. She has some pretty flaky ideas."

My face heated. I didn't think Liberty could hear him, but he'd probably call some of my ideas flaky too. "You mean the interest in aliens?" I whispered back. "She's hardly alone in that, and it draws people to the museum."

"That's the least of it. But I won't be another small-town gossip. I'm sure you'll find out soon enough. See you."

"Okay."

I followed Liberty. She stopped next to the diorama of aliens and a spaceship, which seemed appropriate. When she saw Victor wasn't following us, she said, "I hope that was all right. You didn't look thrilled. I thought you might want an escape."

"What?" My brain started to catch up. "Oh, with Victor. Yeah, I'm happy to get out of the dinner invite. Thanks." I gave a little laugh. "I didn't think you or Elena had said anything about a book club." And I was a loner, so why was I oddly disappointed?

"There is one, and you are invited," Liberty said. "Elena texted me after you were at the sheriff's office today. She said she didn't think to invite you, but I should."

"Oh. That's very nice of her." The embarrassed heat in my face turned to a cozy warmth flowing through my body. I'd never been in a book club, but they sounded nice. A small group, a topic of conversation that wasn't our personal lives, maybe a glass of wine. And friendship? I liked Liberty and Elena. I could get to know them better, slowly and cautiously, and maybe meet a few more women. Not necessarily only women, but it always sounded like book clubs were largely female.

The perfect place to learn more about the town and its inhabitants. I wished I hadn't thought of that. It made me feel sneaky.

"You've got an hour," Liberty said. "I'll text you the address." She pulled out her phone, and I gave her the number. "Don't eat too much first," she said. "We really do have lots of snacks."

"Er, I don't really have anything . . ."

"Don't worry about it. First time's free." Liberty grinned, and we walked out of the museum together before heading our separate ways.

# Chapter Fourteen

AT HOME, I fed the animals, gave and got attention, and ate a bowl of soup since I was hungry and not sure what *snacks* would be available at the meeting. I also searched for information on Reggie Heap. He had an online resume on a job site that showed him as "looking for work" and hadn't been updated with the Banditt Museum position. Starting at age thirty, he'd spent a decade at a government job that was probably hard to lose unless he did something pretty bad. After that, he'd lasted only one to three years at most jobs, with gaps in between. Each move took him to less impressive jobs that likely paid less. That didn't tell me a whole lot, but it fit with the idea that he couldn't behave himself at work.

But was it because of sexual harassment, or general laziness and incompetence? Or had he been involved in something even worse, and companies found it easier to fire him quietly than have him arrested and deal with the negative publicity? Everything I learned about Reggie suggested *pathetic, creepy sad sack* rather than *criminal mastermind.* Now presumably a successful criminal mastermind didn't go around *acting* like one, but I suspected

Reggie got in over his head on something. I just wished I knew what, or at least that it wouldn't come back to bite me too.

That research kept me too busy to talk myself out of going to this book club. At five minutes before seven, I parked outside the address Liberty had given me. Then I sat in the van. The week had already been intense and stressful. Was I really going to expose myself to more new people? A cozy evening at home with my animals sounded much better.

But I'd already turned down one dinner and three lunch invites. If I kept up that pace, there might not be others. I told myself I didn't want others—except I sort of did. Small town, quirky people, a high tolerance for weirdness . . . maybe I could make some casual friendships and have some kind of social life, even if I had to hide my true self. That might be better than nothing.

Also, I might learn something useful here. Thinking about the meeting as a chance to investigate made me feel a little guilty, but it took away the pressure to impress people and make friends. I was simply there to observe, maybe ask a few subtle questions, and learn. If I never got invited back, no big deal.

A figure strode down the sidewalk. It was dark, no streetlights, just porch lights and a little light spilling from windows, but the loose-limbed confidence looked familiar. When I was sure it was Liberty, I got out of the car and met her on the sidewalk.

"Hi." She spoke almost absently, not really looking at me, as if thinking about something else. "Glad you could make it."

"Thanks for inviting me." I was hit by sudden panic. "You really did intend to invite me, right? Because if it was just to save me from Victor . . . I don't want to intrude."

"Elena likes you, and we trust her judgment. Come on."

*Elena* liked me? How did Liberty feel? But it was probably too soon for her to judge. I was still wondering if someone I'd met was a murderer, which was hardly a promising first step to friendship.

Liberty knocked on the door and pushed it open. She led the way to a living room where three women sat on shabby sofas and easy chairs.

Elena popped up like a jack-in-the-box. "Oh good, you made it! Let me introduce you. This is Wilma."

The woman stood and offered her hand. "It's nice to meet you." Her voice was low and husky, very pleasant. She was in her forties, if I'm any judge, which I'm clearly not given how badly I'd guessed Elena's age. Wilma was stocky and about five feet tall, with golden skin and black hair that hung in a smooth sweep, framing her face and just touching her shoulders.

"This is Petra. She's new at the museum." Elena spoke as if that was the most exciting thing to happen in ages. Maybe it was, as far as she knew. She turned to the next woman. "This is Anne Marie."

"Hello. Welcome to Bonneville." Anne Marie was thirtysomething at a wild guess, and very large, maybe four hundred pounds at an even wilder guess. She had a pretty, round face with sweetly curving lips and dark eyes rimmed with purple eyeliner. She wore a low-cut blouse that showed creamy cleavage, and a soft swirling skirt in many shades of purple that I coveted intensely even though I rarely wear skirts.

They asked a few questions about my new job, which I answered without telling them any of the really interesting things that had happened.

"Reggie was an odd duck," Anne Marie said. "My niece works at the gas station. He came in a lot to buy lottery tickets and try to flirt with her. She's seventeen!"

Yeah, that tracked. "Um, he didn't . . . get out of hand, did he?" *Did he behave so badly that someone in your family might kill him?*

"Nah, he'd just hang around being awkward. Maybe not even flirting, really, but taking half an hour to pick out snacks and watching her the whole time. I told her dealing with a pest like that is probably good training for the rest of life, unfortunately."

Everyone grimaced and nodded.

Then Elena said, "Petra recognized one of the WANTED posters we have in the sheriff's office! The man actually came into the museum."

Liberty had been perusing the food set out on a table on

the other side of a large arch. She swung toward me. "When was this?"

"Yesterday. That is, he was at the museum yesterday. I saw the WANTED poster today. Too late to do anything."

"And you're sure this man was wanted?"

"Fairly sure. Not one hundred percent certain." I glanced around at the avid faces. "The sheriff said the guy probably won't come back though."

"It's still exciting." Elena's shrill laugh filled the room. Did she laugh at everything? And did she have to laugh so high-pitched and loud?

"Is that why you went to the sheriff's office?" Liberty asked.

"What? Oh. No." My mind raced. I should've expected the question.

Telling them what I found on Reggie's laptop might lead to questions like how I got into the laptop. I'd lied to Victor about the password because I couldn't explain the truth, but I didn't want to start new friendships by lying if I could avoid it.

"I found Reggie Heap's laptop. Nobody at the museum knew of any close friends or relatives, so, um, I wondered if it would be okay for me to keep it." That was weak but almost accurate.

Liberty eyed me with what I thought was suspicion. "That's very conscientious of you. Did Victor say you could keep it?"

The door creaked open and a woman hurried in with her arms around a big shopping bag.

"Oh, here's Jenny," Elena said.

"Hello everybody! Sorry I'm late." She spoke with a Texas accent.

"You know we won't start without you." Elena laughed. "You bring the wine!"

Jenny was slender, Asian, maybe in her thirties, with glasses and loose, messy hair. Jenny and Elena bustled around opening a wine bottle and filling glasses, which allowed me to ignore Liberty's question, but I had one for her.

"You don't like the sheriff." Okay, that was a statement, not a question. Still, her feelings seemed clear, and I wondered why.

Liberty shrugged. "I just don't trust him. I don't understand him."

"What's to understand?" Wilma asked. "He's a hunk!"

Everyone laughed, except for Liberty, who rolled her eyes.

"He's a good boss," Elena said. "He doesn't care if I have to bring one of the kids for a few hours, and I never worry he's going to hit on me."

"A lack of sexual harassment is a distressingly low bar," Liberty said. "Especially considering that your husband also works for him."

"Maybe," Elena admitted. "Although if you'd worked

some of the places I have . . . Anyway, not every boss will let you bring your kids to the office."

"I'm sure it helps that there are two doors between his office and yours," Liberty said.

"Plus he puts the boys in jail if they're bad." Elena shrieked with laughter as she looked around at us. I expect my face, at least, registered shock. "It's a *joke*. The boys *love* going in the jail cells. Denny got Victor to put him in handcuffs once."

Anne Marie snickered. "So you're teaching your kids that jail is fun. Going for the parent of the year award?"

Elena shrugged. "Dennis and I grew up playing in the arroyos and were never swept away by a flash flood, despite what our mamas and grannies said. Life is full of risks."

"Wine?" Jenny offered me a glass. "Do you drink? It's okay if you don't."

"Um, I don't drink much, but I don't not drink." I took the glass.

"Liberty doesn't like Victor's aura," Jenny said.

"Okay." I wasn't sure what that meant. I looked at Liberty. "You just have a gut feeling about him? Nothing concrete that he's done?"

Liberty sighed and glared at Jenny.

"No, she actually sees auras," Jenny said. "What's Petra's aura like?"

Liberty dropped into an easy chair and leaned back with her legs stretched out. She transferred her glare to her wineglass. "I'm not a party trick."

"But you are at a party," Elena said brightly. "And you're tricky!"

"Besides, it's not fair if you don't share." Jenny looked at me. "Right? I know you're curious too. It's impossible to find out she sees auras and not want to know."

"Um, I guess." Learning that someone else had a gift, or curse, that most people would dismiss was like getting dunked in a cold lake—shocking and my limbs tingled and I couldn't quite breathe. I'd never met anybody else who had psychic or paranormal powers. But then I didn't meet many people. Was I less alone than I'd guessed? If so, why did no one talk about this stuff?

And Jenny was right, now I was wildly curious about my aura—and also terrified. Was my aura good, whatever that meant? Could Liberty see into my mind, my feelings, somehow? Now I knew what it felt like when someone learned about my psychometry. I didn't like it either.

"See?" Jenny turned to Liberty. "It's not fair if you know something about one of us and keep it a secret."

That was a kick to the gut. I was lightheaded and starting to sweat. I sat on the sofa next to Anne Marie and took a sip of wine to give my hands something to do. The wine was tangy and fruity. Not bad. Or maybe very bad, since it would be easy to down a couple of glasses without noticing.

I didn't drink alcohol much, mainly because it was expensive, I was always broke, and I saw no reason to drink alone. But also, I didn't want to lose control and reveal something I'd learned through psychometry. I had to avoid touching people and their belongings, and if I accidentally learned something, I had to remember how I'd learned it so I wouldn't say anything about it. That was tricky enough when sober.

Liberty stared at me. "The question is, do you really want to know? And do you want to hear the truth or something that will make you feel good?"

*Ooh, fun question.*

"How does it work?" I asked to buy some time.

"If you mean scientifically, I have no idea," Liberty said. "I've always been this way. I was ten when I realized not everybody sees auras."

"It's hard to be different." As soon as I said it I regretted letting that slip. "At that age—it must've been strange." *Just guessing here! It's not like I have personal experience with that.*

"Yeah. It doesn't do any harm. It's simply another way brains can work, like synesthesia, when people hear colors or taste shapes. But of course a lot of people don't believe me."

"Chinese medicine says the body has both visible and invisible parts," Jenny said. "Auras are connected to qi, or chakras. Your aura can be different at each chakra."

"All things have energy," Anne Marie said. "We all pick up on it in some way—like that sixth sense that tells you to avoid someone."

Wilma gave a faint snort. "Wish mine worked better. It

might have saved me from a couple of bad exes."

"Does Victor know you can see auras? Is that why . . ." I trailed off. I probably shouldn't tell Liberty what Victor said about her.

"*I* didn't tell him." Liberty raised her eyebrows and looked at Elena.

Elena shook her head. "I wouldn't. You know that."

Liberty's expression softened. "Maybe not on purpose. Things can slip out sometimes."

"I haven't even told Dennis." Elena glanced at me. "My husband, not my son Denny. Well, I mean, I haven't told either of them."

"This is a safe place." Anne Marie's slow, closed-mouth smile suggested she had secrets. But maybe that was just her regular smile.

I looked back at Liberty. "When I asked how it worked, I guess what I meant is, what do you see? Light or colors or . . .?"

What I really wanted to know was how much information she got from auras. Could she tell if someone was a criminal? If they'd done something bad? That could be a powerful talent. Way more useful than mine.

"Glowing colors. For example, Elena tends to have a kind of peach aura. It's brighter when she's happy, and it can shift redder if she's annoyed or frustrated. When she shares her delightful laugh, the colors pulse in time with it." Liberty smiled at Elena in a way that suggested they had shared jokes about her laugh before.

Elena laughed, and I felt guilty. She'd invited me into her home, she was ready to like me based on a few minutes of chatting, and I thought she laughed too loudly? Laughing a lot should be a positive thing.

"Jenny's aura tends to ripple with blue and green," Liberty added. "Anne Marie's aura is interwoven tendrils of blue and turquoise, and tends to be faint, maybe because she's so self-contained. Or not, because I'm just guessing here. Wilma doesn't want to know about hers."

That didn't sound terribly useful. "Do the different colors mean something?"

Liberty shrugged. "Probably. But it's not like I got an instruction manual. Auras change over time, with someone's mood, with their energy level. I can tell if someone's mad or happy, but I can't tell what they've done in the past or guess what they're going to do in the future. It really isn't much more than a party trick."

"Then why don't you like Victor's aura?" Elena asked.

"His is . . . confusing," Liberty said. "Bright colors, green and yellow and red, and big—it takes up a lot of space—which isn't necessarily a bad thing, but I don't like to get too close. It might not mean anything. It just bothers me that I don't know what it means."

"Huh." I wasn't sure whether to be relieved or disappointed. Presumably my aura wasn't horrifying, or Liberty wouldn't have invited me to book club. It didn't sound like she'd be able to identify a murderer though. And her feelings about the sheriff could have meant anything or nothing. I found Victor confusing too, but I hadn't gotten any *bad vibes*. Maybe my sixth sense wasn't very good, or maybe Liberty was being judgmental, like I'd been with Elena's laugh.

I glanced around at the group. "Sorry, I derailed your book club. Maybe we should get started on that." And I could sit quietly, since I hadn't read the book, and avoid the question of my aura for a while longer.

Elena flicked her fingers, brushing away the suggestion. "Oh, book club is just the excuse we used to get together. We talk about the books we've been reading and what we can recommend, but we talk about other stuff too."

"A book club with no homework," Wilma said. "That's how they got me to join. Well, that and food." She got up and headed to the table in the next room, which started a group movement in that direction.

Hadn't Liberty said something about needing me there to help choose the next book, in front of Victor? So she'd lied to him. It seemed risky, given that he knew Elena pretty well. Elena might not tell secrets, but how the book club worked probably wasn't a secret. But maybe Liberty didn't care if Victor caught her in a lie. I'd been cautiously willing to like both of them, and now I didn't know how to feel. Maybe it was simply a matter of two strong personalities that didn't mesh.

We filled plates with cheese and crackers, fruit, tortilla chips, a sour cream dip made with the local green chiles, and cookies.

I looked at my plate full of goodies. "I'm sorry I didn't bring anything."

"Don't worry about it." Elena patted my arm. "We take turns, so you'll have your chance. Besides, we don't yet know whether you bake well or make some special treat, or if we'll have to put you in charge of store-bought snacks or alcohol."

I immediately wanted to start looking up recipes for party food and practicing options for *special treats* to impress them.

For a while the conversation focused on books people had been reading, with other bits of news and general life complaints tossed in. It was a swirl of chatter, more people in one room than I was used to. It felt like far more than six of us.

Which reminded me, where was Haven? Somehow I'd assumed she'd be part of the group. Maybe she had a conflict that night, or didn't get along with another member, or she didn't read much. I didn't ask about her, since the answer might be awkward.

I hadn't figured out how to ask about the guy from the WANTED poster or possible criminal activity in town. I'm not a good enough conversationalist to slip in stuff like that subtly.

Then my phone rang. That happens so rarely that it took

me a moment to recognize the ring tone. I pulled it out and saw Shelley's name. What could she want?

"Sorry, it's my landlord." I stood, planning to go to the next room or outside, and answered.

"Petra? Where are you? I saw you leave, and your car isn't back, but someone's in your house."

## Chapter Fifteen

"THERE SHOULDN'T BE anyone in my house," I said.

"Right. I'll call the police. You get home." She hung up.

The women were all staring at me. "What's wrong?" Elena asked. I wanted to see her question as sympathetic, but I couldn't help feeling she might be more excited about new gossip.

"I need to go." I looked around vaguely before I remembered I hadn't brought anything in with me. "Apparently Shelley, my landlord—but I'll bet you all know her—she said someone is in my house. I live alone," I added, in case my cause for concern wasn't clear. "Well, with my pets, but I don't think she'd mistake a cat or ferret for a person, and the ferrets shouldn't be out of their room . . ." I was rambling. "I have to go."

"I'll go with you." Liberty stood.

"I'll call my husband," Elena said.

"Shelley said she'll call the police," I told her.

"Oh, well, if you want the *police*."

I didn't really care. I just wanted to get home and check

on my animals. What if the intruder opened the cages or the door to the ferret room? What if they let the cats outside? I didn't have anything of value, except for my pets. The thought of losing any of them, or all of them . . . I felt sick.

I stumbled toward the door. Liberty grabbed my arm. "I'll drive. You've had a shock."

I nodded. It wasn't far, and I doubted the streets would be crowded, but I wasn't sure I'd remember how to drive.

"I'll drive Petra in her car, and you can bring me back here," Jenny told Liberty.

We all filed out. Apparently everyone was going to check on the break-in with me. I didn't have enough anxiety left over to worry about that. If this had to do with Reggie's mess, Reggie's death, if he'd left me a situation that caused my pets to be lost or hurt . . . I'd want to kill him myself, if he weren't already dead.

By the time we got to my street two miles away, a police car joined our convoy with its siren wailing and lights flashing. Jenny pulled over to let the police car pass and muttered, "Like they're going to catch anyone while making noise like that."

We pulled up to the very crowded end of the street a minute later. The police car killed the siren and parked behind another marked vehicle. The lights kept flashing, showing the sheriff's symbol on the first car. So it had made a difference for Elena to call her husband.

I looked over at my house. A man strode around the side,

and I gasped. *Intruder!* But he headed toward us, and before I could say anything, he joined the police officer getting out of his car. Probably not a wanted criminal then.

Elena trotted over to them. The man who had come around my house was in a sheriff's uniform, I now saw. He was tall and had dark hair, so for a moment I thought it was Victor. Then he leaned down to kiss Elena. That wasn't terribly professional behavior from someone on duty, but it made a lot more sense from her husband than her boss.

Someone rapped on the driver's side window of my van. I jumped. Jenny rolled down the window.

"Oh, you're not Petra," Shelley's voice said.

I shook myself out of my stupor, got out, and went around the front of the car. Shelley put her hands on my upper arms. I might have tensed at the touch, if I wasn't already so tense, but as long as Shelley didn't take my hands, I wouldn't get another shock. Well, I might get plenty more shocks, given how things had been going, but it wouldn't be from Shelley's giant rings.

"Petra." Her breathing was raspy. "Two men raced out of your house not two minutes ago. I didn't get a good look at them. Usually I like the dark because you can see so many stars. This is the first time I've wished for more security lights. But we've never had trouble before."

Should I apologize? I hadn't brought the trouble—it had been waiting here for me—but Shelley didn't know that.

"I suppose someone thought the house was still empty,"

Shelley said. "Teenagers, maybe, looking for place to party. Oh, I hope they don't have to arrest a former student of mine. That's always so sad."

*Always?* I found my voice. "Did they look like teenagers?"

"Well . . . It's hard to say in the dark."

"You said two men. Are you sure they were men?"

"Hm, I thought so. They seemed built more like men maybe." She looked around at the group gathered there, perhaps noting the wide variety of builds people of any gender could have.

Elena joined us with the two men in uniform. "Petra? This is my husband, Dennis." He was skinnier than Victor and maybe a bit taller, with dark hair but no mustache. They didn't look that much alike up close. "And this is Uberto Gonzalez, with the police."

"Ma'am. Dennis went around the outside of the house and didn't see a sign of anyone still inside." The police officer spoke quickly, maybe claiming his jurisdiction over the sheriff's deputy. "He tried the doors and they're locked. We'd like to check inside and then have you go through to see if anything's missing."

"Of course. Shelley said she saw two men leaving."

Gonzalez nodded to her. "We'll take your statement in a minute, ma'am."

Shelley chuckled. "Don't ma'am me. I put you in time out back in kindergarten!"

He grinned. "That's why I still call you ma'am." To me

he said, "Miss, if you unlock the doors for us . . ."

"How did they get in if the doors are locked?" I spoke mainly to myself as I turned toward the house.

"Could be they jimmied a window," Gonzalez said. "Or someone had a key. Were the locks changed when you moved in?"

I glanced at Shelley, who was right at my side as we went up the path.

"No, I didn't think of it," she said. "But Reggie is dead!"

I pulled my key from my pocket and reached for the door. "Did you get his key back?"

"Yes, the sheriff's office sent it over. I guess they found it . . ." She cleared her throat. "On him."

I flinched and dropped my key. An overreaction, since I'd touched it before and not gotten flashes of Reggie dying in a crash. I was a little unnerved.

"Oh, that's not the key I gave you," Shelley said. "I had copies made. Realized I couldn't count on getting a key back if something happened to my tenant—er, anyway, I wanted a couple more as backup."

Gonzalez retrieved the key and unlocked the door. He started to push it open.

"Wait! I have cats. And ferrets and guinea pigs and rats. The guinea pigs and rats should be in their cages, and the ferrets should be in the second room, but if the intruders opened the door—and the cats could be anywhere."

Someone behind me whispered, "*Rats?*" People were

learning a lot more about me than I'd intended to share.

"Got it." Gonzalez eased the door open and slipped through.

Elena's husband went in after him. "Please stay here." Dennis closed the door behind him.

The rest of us stood on the stoop or in the yard nearby. I still felt numb, like I was stumbling through fog. I wished I hadn't had any wine. But it probably wasn't the wine.

Why would someone be in my house? If it was simply because I was new in town and they wanted to see what I had worth stealing, it would make more sense to wait until after my stuff was delivered. Okay, maybe a potential thief wouldn't know my stuff hadn't been delivered, but everyone in town seemed to know everything, and besides, a peek through the windows would have shown very little in the house.

Plus, random strangers in my house, right when so much else was going on? That would be another unlikely coincidence.

So who was it? Had Liberty invited me to book club to get me out of the house? Was Haven not at book club because she was searching my house? I didn't want to suspect the coworkers who could become friends, but I had to accept the possibility.

Who else knew I would be gone? Victor, I'd already found Reggie's laptop and turned it in. If he found something suspicious on the laptop and wanted to look for more evidence, he could ask me.

Shelley had seen me leave, and we had only her word that the intruders existed. But in that case, why call to tell me someone had been in my house? Unless she wanted to cover up her own thefts, but she certainly knew how little I had and that more would be coming in a day or two.

If any of the possibilities made sense, I couldn't see it.

The door opened. Dennis said, "You can come in now."

I stepped inside, scanning the room for the cats. "Did you see any animals?"

"Just the guinea pigs in cages. You said the ferrets were supposed to be loose, right? One room has open cages. We checked that no one was in the room—no human—and closed the door again."

"Thanks." I headed for the kitchen and stood on a chair. Onyx and Amber crouched on top of the refrigerator. "Oh thank goodness. It's okay, sweeties. Mama's here." I let them sniff my hand, gave Amber a gentle chin rub, and stepped down from the chair.

Dennis looked bemused. "I'm embarrassed we missed them, but we didn't think to look up there."

"It's their safe space," I said. "That's two out of three cats." But not Jet, and he was the most social, the one I would expect to greet me at the door.

Dennis followed me out the other kitchen doorway to the hallway. A quick check showed the rats were still in their closed cages, hidden in a hammock. It took longer to find the ferrets, since I didn't know where their current favorite napping spots were. They all turned up in piles of bedding, looking sleepy but healthy. I breathed a little easier.

"There's a cat out here!" Shelley's voice called from the front room.

I hurried out to find the entire book club there along with Shelley and the police officer. I hadn't imagined they would all follow me in, but of course they would. I should have asked them to stay outside. And maybe barricaded the door as an extra precaution.

At least they were clustered in that one room, and Jet had come out to investigate. He was weaving in between people as Elena followed, bent over trying to pet him.

I was able to take a deep breath for the first time since Shelley's call. "The animals are all here."

"What did they take?" Jenny frowned at the minimal furnishings, just the sofa and a coffee table in that room.

"This is how I left it. Most of my belongings are still on a truck. I don't own anything valuable anyway."

I felt bad adding that last sentence. It's not like I really suspected any of this group of trying to steal from me, probably. But news traveled quickly in this town, so I might as well spread the word that I wouldn't have any valuables even after my pod arrived.

"That's lucky," Gonzalez said. "You might want to upgrade your security anyway."

I hugged myself. "Did you figure out how they got in?"

"The back door was locked, but it looks like you could break in with a credit card," he said. "There was some dirt tracked in there. Nothing clear like a footprint, but my guess is the intruders just jimmied the back door. I take it you didn't use the dead bolt."

"No, I didn't realize I needed to. I'll start."

"What a terrible way to welcome you to town," Shelley said. "I'm so sorry."

"Not your fault," I said automatically. Maybe my landlord could have prevented the break-in with better security. Maybe not though. It would have been worse if they'd broken a window. And if this was related to Reggie's death, and not just random thieves taking advantage of my location at the end of a dark street . . . I didn't want to pursue that thought.

"I'm glad you were home to see the intruder," I added. That was one advantage to having a snoopy landlord living so close.

"Me too." Shelley put one hand to her chest. "And I'm glad I have Toby. No one will bother *me* with him in the house." She gasped. "Do you think the intruders got into my shed?"

"What's in your shed?" Gonzales asked.

"Oh, fifty years of life. Extra furniture and so on. I moved a bunch of Reggie's stuff over there, the things I haven't gotten around to donating yet. Nothing too valuable, but I don't like the idea of someone poking around my things."

"You check it out," Gonzales said to Dennis. "I'll take Miss Shelley's statement."

"Watch out for the black widows," Shelley told Dennis.

"Black widow spiders?" I cringed.

"They're more afraid of you than you are of them," Shelley said.

"If you say so," I mumbled.

"It's the scorpions you want to watch out for." Liberty winked at me, but I couldn't tell if it was a *That's a joke* wink or a *You'll get used to living with things that want to kill you* wink.

"It's the house centipedes I don't like." Elena gave a theatrical shudder. "All feathery with too many legs. I know their venom isn't very toxic, and they compete for territory with the real centipedes, which have a very painful bite. But the way they move is creepy, and they're fast!"

"Millipedes are cool," Wilma said. "They're toxic, but chickens can eat them."

I might have whimpered.

Gonzales cleared his throat. "Mind if Miss Shelley and I sit at your kitchen table?"

"That's fine." The benefit of talking about toxic pests was that having strangers in my house no longer seemed so bad.

"Dennis, you look around that shed." As he headed to the kitchen, he added under his breath, "I don't care how many creepy crawlies there are."

Elena was sitting on the floor with Jet in her lap. She glanced up at her husband and whispered, "Ooh, he's letting you do something!"

He snickered, shushed her, and glanced around at us. "Sometimes the police are a little territorial. It's fine. Oh, I'll ask Miss Shelley if she has any scrap wood I can use to make some doorstops and bars for the windows. I can do that after I check her shed." He headed for the kitchen.

"Thank you," I called after him. I don't know how I sounded. Probably as dazed as I felt. But it was a nice gesture, and I was glad he'd thought of it. It would make me feel safer. Maybe the intruders had found what they wanted, or searched well enough that they knew it wasn't in the house. But maybe they'd heard distant sirens or noticed Shelley watching them from her window. If they got scared off partway through their search, they might be back.

I shivered. Maybe I should get a dog soon. A big one, like Toby. But I'd want a sweet, goofball dog, the kind that would greet strangers with a wagging tail, not to mention one small enough I could afford to feed it. Could I train a dog to be friendly and also a guard dog?

I looked at the group of women who remained in my front room, standing around the one sofa piled with blankets covered in cat hair. "I'm sorry I ruined your book club."

"Are you kidding?" Elena beamed. "This is the most excitement we've had since my step-grandmother tried to exorcise a ghost."

I could not think of a thing to say to that.

"I should grab some glasses before they start that interview," Jenny said. "Unless you don't have any?"

"There are some in the cupboard next to the refrigerator. But I don't have anything to offer you to drink." Also, I was kind of assuming they would leave now.

Jenny pulled a bottle of wine out of a canvas bag slung over her shoulder. "I got you covered. Thought you might need something for the shock." She headed to the kitchen. Liberty went with her.

"Can I see your rats?" Anne Marie asked. "I love rats. I had one in high school."

"I've never seen a ferret before," Wilma hinted.

"Okay. I guess . . . come meet the family." I led the way down the hallway. Apparently I was having a spontaneous housewarming party. This still ranked as the strangest week I'd ever had, but at least it wasn't all bad.

# Chapter Sixteen

DENNIS REPORTED NO sign of a break-in at Shelley's shed. He went through my house putting sturdy sticks in every window frame so the windows wouldn't open unless you removed the wood pieces from the inside. He also found or whittled some triangular pieces I could use as doorstops to jam the doors closed when I was inside. Shelley said she'd pay for dead-bolt locks on both doors, the kind you could lock from the outside, not just when you were home. Anne Marie had tools and offered to install the locks.

After the police officer finished with Shelley, we went to her shed and grabbed more chairs. Shelley joined the party. And it was a party by that point, because Liberty and Elena ran back to Elena's house to get the food.

Nobody asked me about any of this, in case you're wondering. I was certainly wondering why we didn't just go back to Elena's house, where she already had comfortable seating and snacks laid out. But when everyone finally left, and I tumbled into bed (or sofa), I realized I wasn't afraid to sleep in the house. Any bad mojo the intruders left behind had been wiped out by the positive energy of seven fabulous females. (I'm counting myself and Shelley, if you're doing the math.)

I had two glasses of wine over several hours, which shouldn't cause a hangover, but I also stayed up too late and ate way too much of the hot fudge cake Liberty whipped up in my kitchen. (She'd grabbed the ingredients and a pan from Elena's kitchen when they ran back over there.) The desert had a very moist cake layer with chocolate pudding on top, served warm with whipped cream, so I could see why she'd made it fresh and why she called it *therapy cake*. It was shockingly good, but I don't normally eat that much sugar in a week, so it could explain the headache and vaguely queasy feeling I had in the morning.

The next day, I got to work a few minutes late. Peyton was behind the front counter, helping a sunburned family that already looked tired. "Petra! Wait a moment, please."

When your boss tells you to hold, you hold. Well, maybe it depends on what he's asking you to hold, but I paused, fairly certain he wasn't going to berate me for my tardiness.

Peyton gave the visitors a map and came around the counter to me. "Petra, my dear." He put his left hand on my shoulder. "I heard about your break-in last night. I trust you are all right."

"Yes, thank you."

Something glinted golden at the edge of my vision. The cuff on his Western-style shirt had pulled up past a watch on his left wrist. I raised my hand and put it over his wrist—

over the watch, really, but I hoped the gesture would seem like appreciation for his support.

"It was a shock." I forced my eyes open when they wanted to flutter closed so I could see the visions better. "I suppose someone wondered if the new kid in town had a lot of valuable electronics or something." I hoped what I was saying made sense.

"Please don't hold it against the town, or the museum." He squeezed my shoulder, looking grandfatherly and kind, which wasn't quite the truth.

"I don't." I dropped my hand and he removed his. From me, I mean, not from his arm.

"You're not going to let it run you out of town?"

I smiled. "You won't get rid of me that easily."

"Good, good. Shelley said your storage container should come this week. Let me know if you need help. I'll send Kit."

"Thanks." I was hardly even surprised at the speed of the grapevine now. "There's no rush, so I'll probably wait until my days off to deal with it."

"Don't overwork yourself, my dear. I expect a lot from my employees, but I want you to be happy here." That was true.

"Thanks. I think I will be. I'm excited about what I can do with the place."

I pondered what I'd learned as I turned down the hall to the breakroom. Coffee was a necessity this morning.

Peyton must have worn that watch for something like

fifty years, and it told me a lot about him. He was shrewd, determined, more than a little vain. He could shift between grandfatherly and good old boy as his audience required. He'd definitely take a good deal if he could get it, and he wasn't above flattering people or pretending their antiques weren't as valuable as they actually were. After all, if they didn't bother to research it, he wasn't obligated to point it out. But he'd accept a fair deal cheerfully enough—which I should keep in mind for negotiating raises in the future.

I hadn't felt any real harm in Peyton, and if he was innocent, Gloria almost certainly was as well. Kit . . . I didn't know much about him, except he had a superficial charm which could hide almost anything underneath. He didn't seem like the type to be involved in sex trafficking, but I could imagine him removing items from the museum without his grandfather's knowledge and selling them. I couldn't see why he'd involve Reggie Heap though, let alone kill him. I could also see him turning the museum into a drug drop, probably for the excitement as much as the money, living up to his adventurous name. But a drug ring would involve outsiders and might turn shockingly bad.

Speaking of, Kit stepped out of the breakroom. "Hey! I'm sorry about your break-in last night. That's not a good welcome to our town."

"Thanks. Who told you about it?"

"It was the talk of the break room." He chuckled. "The talk of the break room was your break-in."

I didn't laugh.

"Haven was sorry she missed the party afterward." He grinned. "I am too. Sounds like quite a night."

Okay, Liberty must have talked about it, since she was the only person from the museum there last night. She'd either made it sound like nonstop fun, or Kit was one of those guys who thought a women-only party involved pillow fights in skimpy negligee. And if Liberty had been talking about last night in the break room, then book group wasn't a secret from Haven. Good, because apparently nothing stayed secret for long. That was something to ponder later.

I felt like I should ask Kit questions, but I couldn't think of any I could actually ask.

*Got any idea who would break into my house, or more to the point break into Reggie's former house? Do you think they were looking for the computer I already turned in at the sheriff's office, which suggests sex was the key, one way or the other? Or would I have found more clues to his murder if I hadn't focused on the porn problem?*

Yeah, I wasn't going to say any of that. He wasn't wearing a watch or rings, which was just as well because I couldn't think of an excuse to touch him that wouldn't send the wrong message.

"Is there any coffee left?" I asked.

"We can make more. It'll get drunk." He chuckled. "Like y'all last night, it sounds like. I'll show you how the coffee maker works."

He showed me where they kept the coffee and set the

next pot to brewing as I watched what he did. Then he leaned against the counter as the coffee maker grumbled. Great, now I had to wait until the coffee brewed, and apparently he planned to keep me company. He asked a few questions about the break-in, and I explained my new security. When I started, I thought it would be good to let people know I had security now. But halfway through I realized I might be providing intel that would let someone get around that minimal security. Pieces of wood might keep the windows from lifting open, but they wouldn't keep someone from breaking a window.

At least the awkward delay gave me time to come up with some questions I could ask Kit.

"I found the case keys on my desk yesterday. I had no idea who left them until the sheriff came in and told me. I thought maybe a ghost had returned them after borrowing them." I smiled to suggest that was a joke.

"I wouldn't put anything past this place, but as far as I know we don't have ghosts. We have artifacts used in shootouts, but no grisly murders or sudden deaths with unfinished business took place in the museum itself."

*That's what you think.*

"I'm just glad the sheriff returned the keys, so we didn't have to call a locksmith," I said. "I suppose you have keys to all the offices and rooms." I put subtle emphasis on *you.*

I know, I hadn't actually asked a question yet, but I was trying to figure out how to say, *Why did you go into my office uninvited and could you please not?*

Kit's gaze shifted away from me. "There's a spare set of all the door keys in the office."

He didn't say he'd *used* those.

"I hope those are kept secure," I said, "both so no one can steal them and so you can find them if someone loses theirs."

"Well, they live on the hook in the office. As long as they get returned there, we can find them. Only my folks and I have keys to the main office."

"Good." So only the Banditt family could get into any room of the museum. The curators should only have keys to their own sections, although someone might borrow the master keys, and then they could have copies made.

The coffee was starting to drip, so I found a mug and put a splash of half-and-half in it. When that was done, the coffeepot was still only half full.

"If I pull the pot out, will it stop long enough to pour a cup?" I asked.

"Yeah, it might drip a bit but the main flow should shut off."

I filled my cup. "Thanks for letting me get the first cup." I scurried out, leaving Kit behind.

As I wandered through the museum, I looked for cameras (real or fake) and studied the doors. I hadn't gotten a key to the museum itself, but Peyton had given me a key to the back door so I could go in and out from my wing. Maybe

Liberty and Haven had similar access. If I came in the back door after hours, I could get out of the geology wing, since I controlled that access door. From there I could get to certain other parts of the museum, since some of the hallways and big rooms, like the one with the wagons and old cars, didn't have doors to close. I couldn't access the front office or certain other rooms. I could get into the gift shop, since it was off to one side of the front counter, with no wall to separate it. Assuming Reggie had the same backdoor key, he could've done all that as well.

Did that tell me anything useful? Not that I could see, but at least I was learning my way around the museum.

I got to my office, sat for a minute, and almost collapsed under the weight of everything I had to do.

I grabbed the workroom key. No tourists would bother me back there, and probably no one from the museum would seek me out. Plus sorting through the new donation sounded more fun than anything else on my list. Unless, of course, I discovered something that got Reggie killed and made myself a target.

Because it seemed like people were looking for something. Fausto Yubeta had been hanging around the geology wing. Why? Two people broke into my house last night and took nothing as far as I knew. What had they been hoping to find? Or had they found something hidden that I'd missed while searching for pet escape routes? Were they looking for Reggie's computer or something else?

Maybe knowing the answers would make me a target, but I already felt like one. What if the intruders came back while I was home and demanded I give them the thing? I wasn't even safe in the museum. All someone would have to do is wait until the geology wing was empty of other visitors, which was ninety percent of the time. Close the door to the wing, and most visitors wouldn't try to go through it. No one else in the museum would hear me scream.

Having thoroughly freaked myself out, I left a sticky note on my office door that said, IN WORKROOM so no one could accuse me of hiding. (I was actually hiding.) I debated adding my phone number, but practically everyone I knew already had it: the Banditts, Shelley, Liberty, and now both the sheriff and police.

I stepped out the back door, propping it with the rock. If I left the workroom door open too, I'd be able to see this door and anyone who came out of it. It was cool, only sixty degrees when I left home, but the day's high was forecast at seventy-three, with plenty of sun, so the air flow would be nice too.

I started sorting the box Reggie had left on the table. It still seemed weird taking over from a dead man, especially given the way he died. But I needed the job, and I couldn't come up with a good excuse for simply ignoring the big new donation forever. Anyway, if the killer hadn't gotten what they wanted, I needed to find it, and hopefully evidence that would convince the police Reggie had been murdered. I'd be safer with that information out, especially if I found whatever the killer wanted, told everyone, and had it put someplace safe.

I tried to focus on the box of rocks to distract myself from all those thoughts. It didn't entirely work, but I did eventually sink into the job of identifying and sorting what I had: some samples of interest to geologists, but nothing that would get anyone killed. It would take me months to get through all of the boxes stuffed onto the deep, ten-foot-long shelves at the back of the workroom.

Nothing to do but keep swimming, or in this case, keep sorting.

By noon I had three piles: things for display (well, it was one piece of Smithsonite—a frothy, seafoam-green mineral from a New Mexico mine—so not really a *pile*), small mineral samples to sell in the museum gift shop, and larger rocks and minerals that might get a decent price from collectors.

Now what? The storage room didn't exactly have acres of free space for the three sets. I had enough table space to keep going for a while, as long as none of the other curators wanted to use the room, but eventually I'd have to come up with a different solution.

I got up to stretch. I needed more boxes and some packing material. Then I could pack up the *sell to collectors* items and stack those boxes under the workroom table or in my office. Once I had enough, I'd have a good excuse to go to a rock, gem, and mineral show. I could get rid of some of the overflow stock, see more of the Southwest, and call it work.

I could love this job.

The room had gotten a little warmer, but I was chilled from sitting still, my coffee long gone. The open door beckoned, the sunlight so bright I had to blink away spots if I looked at it for too long. It was tempting to head outside, maybe even get lunch, since I'd skipped breakfast. But if I took lunch this early, I'd have a longer afternoon. Besides, if I waited an hour, it would warm up even more and I could eat outside in the sunshine.

I headed for the back of the workroom to scowl at the remaining boxes. There were so many. Any one of them could still hold a secret, or the secret might be someplace else entirely, or it might not even exist. Maybe Reggie had been killed because someone thought he'd found, I don't know, an old treasure map, but the treasure was a myth.

The light changed. I swung around. Someone stood in the workroom doorway haloed by the sunlight behind. I tried to convince myself it was Peyton or Kit. Even Victor or Officer Gonzalez. But the silhouette wasn't tall enough. And he wasn't shaped like Haven or Elena. It was a slender man. Familiar in a way that sent prickles jumping through my limbs as my lungs seized up. We were alone in the workroom, no one else close enough to hear a yell.

Fausto Yubeta stepped into the room and shut the door behind him.

# Chapter Seventeen

HIS MOUTH MOVED, but I couldn't hear him through the buzzing in my head. My phone was over where I'd been sitting—much closer to him than to me. He wasn't a big guy; I probably outweighed him. But I had no fighting experience. No weapon.

He studied me, frowning slightly. Maybe because I'd frozen like a prey animal, immobile as its brain scrambled to make sense of a threat. Forget fight or flight. I couldn't move a muscle. Maybe if I managed to fall over, I could play dead.

*Great plan, Petra!*

He placed his hands palms-down on the table. "I didn't mean to frighten you. But if you know anything that could help . . ."

He wasn't holding a weapon. He was asking for information. If I could get down there to my phone, maybe I could dial 911 surreptitiously while distracting him with conversation.

*Better plan. Really fun. (eye roll)*

I managed to swallow. Then to move my mouth. "Sorry, can you start over?"

"I am looking for my brother. He disappeared at least a week ago, maybe two. I followed his trail here."

"Your brother." My mind still wasn't working well, but I managed to take a couple of steps forward. I didn't allow myself to glance at my precious phone.

"Yes. Have you seen him?" He spoke softly, his English clear but accented. "He looks a lot like me."

I paused again, studying him. "What's your name?"

"Macario Yubeta."

My body went hot and then cold and then hot again, like it couldn't decide how to react to that. "Macario—not Fausto?"

His face lit up. "You know him?"

I shook my head rapidly. "I only moved here a couple of days ago." I shouldn't have admitted recognizing the name. Now I needed a reason for it. "I saw his picture."

Should I mention *where* I saw his picture? He'd know I knew Fausto was a criminal. But I didn't want this man to think I knew more about Fausto than I did—like what he'd been doing and where he was now.

"Can you prove you're not him?" I asked.

He reached his hand around to a back pocket. I held my breath until he set a wallet on the table. He pulled out an ID card and slid it in my direction. I had to come forward fifteen feet to see it clearly. And then I had to take my gaze off of him, which might be the hardest thing I've ever done.

I looked down. The ID, from Mexico, said MACARIO

YUBETA. It didn't prove anything. It might be fake. Fausto might be a middle name or nickname.

But if this man was actually Fausto, I couldn't figure out what he was trying to accomplish. If he wasn't, I might learn something from him. Well, if he *was* Fausto, I might learn even more, but I'd take less knowledge in exchange for no criminals in the room with me.

Unless Macario was *also* a criminal.

I looked up. Macario retrieved the license and returned it to his wallet. I should have touched it. Maybe I wouldn't have learned anything, and I would have felt incredibly vulnerable trying to see a vision and keep an eye on him too, but I should have taken the chance.

Now I had choices. I could deny all knowledge, hope he believed me, and get out of there as quickly as possible. But given my presumably terrified expression in response to seeing anyone with the name Yubeta, it might be hard to pull off claiming I didn't know anything. I didn't, really, but I could hardly prove that.

Or did I know something? "You said your brother disappeared a week or two ago."

He nodded. "He came north on . . . business." He hesitated over the word, and I didn't think he was unsure of the English. He knew his brother's *business* might have gotten him in trouble. "He was due back over a week ago. When he didn't return, eventually his wife called me."

"His *wife*?" I don't know why that surprised me so

much. Criminals could have wives or be wives.

"She is worried he is with another woman. I am worried he is in trouble. I know he came here, and he had a contact at the museum, a man called Reggie. But Reggie is no longer here."

"How do you know all that?"

"In Mexico, I am a journalist."

I sank onto the stool I'd been using before. My mind was making up for lost time by racing. Fausto Yubeta disappeared at least a week ago—maybe two, which would be around the time Reggie died. I flashed back to the image from the crystal clusters. One person on the ground. One person holding the rock. The sense of shock and something like pride. Was that Fausto? Would a criminal be shocked at his own violence?

He was wanted for violent crimes, but that didn't mean he'd committed murder before. The first time might be a shock even for a violent man. But if Fausto had killed Reggie, where did Fausto go? Not home to his wife. He might have many reasons for that, but would he also not contact his brother or any of his family? Would he hang around and break into my house?

"Did you break into my house last night?" I asked.

"I—no—someone broke into your house?" His confusion looked real, for what that's worth.

"Okay, never mind that for now." I studied him again. I wasn't entirely convinced he wasn't the man on the poster.

But the more I looked at him, the more I thought he might not be. Did this man really look a little different, beyond the superficial, like facial hair? Or was I rewriting my memory in order to feel safe?

He had his hands back on the table. I didn't think he was keeping them in sight by accident. He was trying not to scare me. (Not doing a great job of it, what with surprising me when I was alone in an outbuilding, but he looked enough like his criminal brother that he'd want to avoid people.)

He wore a simple band like a wedding ring, and a watch that looked old, early twentieth century. Maybe an inherited heirloom.

I cleared my throat. "This is going to sound strange, but may I take your hand for a moment?"

His eyes widened. After a few seconds, he held out his right hand.

"Um, the other one," I said.

He looked like he wanted to back out of the room. Maybe acting irrational—or, you know, like my regular self—is a better defense than knowing martial arts. But he held out the hand with the ring and watch.

If everything he said was true, he might be wary of me. From his point of view, his brother disappeared, Reggie disappeared, and I was here.

I imagined Shelley saying, *He's more afraid of you than you are of him.*

Not likely!

I slid my left hand into his but stopped when my fingertips rested on his ring, so only our fingers were touching. I placed my right hand on the back of his hand, my fingers resting just short of his watch. It was probably the weirdest handshake he'd ever experienced. It would be in my top five as well.

My eyes fluttered closed as the images hit.

*Love. Adoration. Years of affection, turning to each other in times of grief and exhaustion. And still that initial spark of "I'm the luckiest man alive" from his wedding day.*

Criminals could have wives.

I stretched the fingers of my right hand to touch the watch.

*Worry. So much responsibility. Always helping others, always struggling to survive. Also some pride—in his work, his family. And despair that he could not do enough. Hurt that his younger brother made bad choices again and again, despite everything the family had done for him.*

Older feelings lingered, faint, merely whispers of hard work and joy and grief. But the feelings from the ring matched the stronger, more recent feelings from the watch. They belonged to the same person. I didn't think the man who'd infused his ring and watch with all that could be a bad person.

But what if this man had recently taken those items from someone else? Could I be reading emotions from the wrong person?

I opened my eyes. He was looking at me with a strange

expression, something like fascination. The moment hummed between us. A connection, unexpected but warm.

I can't pretend I'm the best at reading other people, separate from their things. But everything I'd picked up from this man made more sense as a worried older brother than a dangerous criminal.

I released his hand. Ideas swirled as everything I thought I knew shifted into a new pattern. I was close to understanding some of it, but I needed more information, more proof. And that meant I would have to reveal parts of myself I preferred to hide.

I would have to trust.

I cleared my throat and forced out a word. "Okay."

"You know something? You will help me?"

I nodded, but my trust had limits. "I have some ideas, but I need to contact a friend first." I picked up my phone.

"Do you wish me to wait outside?" he asked.

"No, it's all right." I was already texting Liberty: *Come to the workroom outback ASAP, please. Alone.*

I looked at Macario Yubeta. At least I was fairly confident that's who I was looking at. My thoughts ricocheted. Ideas were fine, but I needed information. Proof of what had happened.

"Actually, yes," I said. "I need to go to my office for a minute. I'll close up here."

I grabbed my phone, rinsed my coffee mug at the sink, and ushered him out. I locked the door behind us.

Macario watched me with a wry smile. "You are not running to call the police on me, I pray."

I gave a weak chuckle. "No. What would I tell the police?"

He glanced around the museum yard. "Well, I believe I may be trespassing."

"I suppose, but I left the door open. Did you come through the museum?" He was lucky I hadn't shown his brother's WANTED poster to everyone.

"No, I saw someone leave through the gate." He pointed to the back gate with the padlock. "He did not turn the numbers on the lock afterward."

"It was a man?" That was a relief. I'd been pretty sure I always turned the dials on the lock after I left. The combination lock wasn't much good if you didn't actually lock it.

He nodded. "The younger man with the beard."

Kit then. Sloppy of him.

"You were in the museum the other day watching me. You didn't say anything, ask any questions."

"I had called the museum office. They said they knew nothing about Fausto and the man Reggie was dead. I did not know how you fit into this. I wanted to observe you first."

"I guess I can understand that," I said slowly. "But, you know, I was at the sheriff's office and saw a poster of your brother. I . . . might've told the sheriff I saw him here, when I had seen you."

"I spoke to the police when I first arrived two days ago." He grimaced. "It took some time to convince them I was not my brother. I thought it best to stay out of sight after that."

So he'd spoken to the police, but not the sheriff. Had Victor talked to the police after I'd said I saw a wanted criminal? It seemed like a logical thing to do—if Victor had believed me, and if they didn't keep secrets from each other because they were—what was the word Dennis had used? Territorial?

"I slept in that vehicle last night." Macario pointed at a long car that I would inexpertly identify as a 1970s sedan. The paint had faded to an unappetizing purple brown, the tires were flat, and it was missing a bumper.

"Comfy."

"I wanted to keep my eyes on things."

"Right."

The door from the geology wing swung farther open. Liberty took a step through and stopped, one hand still on the door, looking from Macario to me. "Everything all right?"

"You were fast." And I'd gotten caught in conversation and hadn't done what I had intended. "I'm fine. Um. This is Macario Yubeta. I'm sorry to put you on the spot, but . . . can you tell anything about him?"

Macario looked puzzled. "We have never met."

But Liberty gave me a shrewd glance. Then she squinted at Macario. "It's bright out here. Come inside."

"Is the room empty?" I asked.

"It's safe." Liberty held the door for us. Inside, she studied Macario again. "Am I looking for anything in particular?"

The poor man stood against the wall, his expression like someone surrounded by dogs that might be friendly or might bite.

"It's a long story," I said, "and I'll tell it all, but . . . First I'd like to be sure I'm not making a mistake in believing him, trusting him."

"It doesn't exactly work that way, but I don't see anything that tells me to be afraid."

I sucked in a deep breath and let it out. Apparently I'd still been more anxious than I'd realized. "Good."

"I have questions," Macario said.

I pointed at him. "All of this is off the record. Do you have that term? You can't write about us."

"You have my word. If you help me find my brother, I will be in your debt."

"Please explain to Liberty—oh, this is Liberty—what you told me. I have to do something in my office."

# Chapter Eighteen

I CLOSED MY office door behind me. Even though the door was mostly glass, I felt slightly more secure. My heart galloped as if I'd been running—but it was my mind that raced.

I looked at the fluorite crystals. I didn't need to touch them again to remember the vision. Someone lying on the floor, legs in jeans. The person holding the crystal . . . No physical image of them, but I had the emotion. Shock at what they'd done, a little pride.

I'd assumed Reggie was the victim. He seemed the type who would become a victim—a moody loner, his career stalled, winding up here because he'd been kicked out of other jobs. Someone who could be pushed around, with no real friends to offer advice or help.

Wait a minute. *Moody loner with no real friends* could apply to me. There was a lesson there, but I'd ponder it later.

Anyway, would a violent criminal have been shocked and excited at his own violence?

Maybe Fausto wouldn't. But Reggie might. That idea changed everything.

I dropped to my hands and knees. I'd avoided touching the carpet where the body had lain, because it was nothing I wanted to experience, and the clues pointed to Reggie as the victim. His office, he was dead. But if that was wrong, and if the person had been alive when they fell, the carpet might still retain some emotion—it might hold an important clue.

The victim had fallen along one side of my desk. I edged toward the area, lightheaded. I dragged in air and the feeling receded. I could do this. I had to do this. I had stepped into Reggie's job, his home. If I did not want to repeat his life and death, I needed to know what happened.

I sat on my heels and reached for the area where the body had fallen. Would the intensity of the emotion be strong enough to leave residue, when the emotion hadn't lasted very long? Would I find anything beyond pain or fear?

At first I got nothing strong enough to identify. With my eyes closed, I felt around the area with both hands. My fingertips brushed a spot where the carpet felt different. Crusty. I flinched in disgust but then the emotions flooded me.

A flash of surprise. Not even anger or fear, he was so startled.

Behind that . . . I picked up a kind of cold satisfaction. Vanity wasn't quite the right word. He liked being in control. He deserved to have everything he wanted. He would take it, and he would feel nothing for anyone he hurt. Even in the last moments of his life, he didn't believe someone could challenge him and win.

My gorge rose. I sat back and crossed my arms over my chest, my hands in fists. I didn't want to touch anything until I washed them. I suspected the crusty area was blood. But not Reggie's. Fausto Yubeta had pushed someone too far. *Poor Reggie* had snapped and fought back. He must have taken Fausto's body to the mountains to hide it. Then Reggie had, after all, died of natural causes—a heart attack brought on by the physical and mental stress of what he'd done.

I felt queasy, and a little guilty. I should have explored the carpet sooner. Blood would help prove what had happened.

But no, even if I'd pointed out the spot to the sheriff, or someone, it was hardly enough to set off an investigation. People had accidents and bled. No one was going to test a spot of dried blood on some carpet without a lot more evidence that a crime had been committed. And no one knew Fausto Yubeta had died at all. Only his brother suspected the man's disappearance meant something.

A tap on the door behind me jolted me out of my thoughts. I put one forearm on the desk, heaved myself upright, and turned. Liberty and Macario looked at me through the glass.

Liberty half smiled and opened the door. "You okay?"

I nodded. "Well, actually no." I grabbed disinfecting wipes to clean my hands. "I mean, I'm okay, but not—

Macario, I might know what happened to your brother, but I can't prove it. I think we need to go out to the mountain where Reggie Heap died. Liberty, will you come too?"

Her gaze narrowed. "You don't want me to look at more auras. Not out there."

"Only if you think you can pick up auras a couple of weeks after someone died. But no, I'm asking you as a friend." I thought I could trust Macario. I trusted Liberty more, and I didn't want to do this alone. I couldn't exactly say that out loud, but I tried to say it with my eyes.

Liberty nodded once. "Okay, I'll drive. But I think you have some explaining to do."

We headed outside to Liberty's car, where I claimed the backseat. This would be hard enough without them looking at me.

Of course, as Liberty pulled out of the parking lot, Macario twisted to look at me. "This is very strange," he said. "You seem like nice people, but I would like to know what it is about."

"Yeah." I took a deep breath. "It's going to sound strange. You're not going to like it."

"It is already very strange, and I have heard many things I do not like. Life is full of disappointments. Pretending they do not exist does not help."

I nodded. "Okay. The thing is, I sometimes . . ."

It had been years since I'd told anyone about this. The words didn't want to come out.

"I can pick up an object and get images from its history," I said in a rush. "From the people who used it or wore it or whatever."

"I've heard of that," Liberty said. "Not telekinesis, that's moving objects with your mind. Psych—psych something."

"Psychometry, and if you know that much, it's more than most people."

Macario was studying my face as if he could see through to the brain inside. I didn't know where to look.

"Anyway, when I got here—when I started this job—I cleaned up the office." I realized I was rubbing my forearm.

"And you found something strange?" Liberty asked.

"You could say that. I picked up one of the rocks from the shelves. I wear gloves sometimes, so I won't get so much information. It's distracting, and it can hurt. I wasn't wearing gloves for that, because I figured those rocks were just on display, not something people wore or used, like a watch, or an old miner's headlamp—you wouldn't catch me touching one of those."

The words were flowing now, like they'd been pushing against a dam all this time. I tried to rein in my babbling. "So I picked up a sample of fluorite—purple crystals. I got this flash of violence. An image of somebody holding the rock, and a body on the floor."

I couldn't look at Macario, but even from my peripheral vision, the intensity of his gaze was unnerving. I was squeezing my forearm so hard it hurt.

"Did you tell anyone?" Liberty asked.

"How could I? Who would believe me?"

"Well, you got us in this car, heading out to the site of Reggie's crash," she said.

"Yeah. Thanks. But I didn't know you then, and I didn't meet Macario until now." I forced myself to meet his gaze. "I thought at first Reggie was the victim. When I saw your brother on a WANTED poster, I figured he'd killed Reggie and staged the accident. But now I think that's wrong. I think Reggie was the one holding the rock."

No one spoke for a few seconds. Finally Macario said slowly, "You think my brother was the body on the floor."

I nodded. "I don't know what they were up to. I don't know what happened to your brother. Maybe he didn't die. Maybe he got away."

"That does not seem likely," Macario said. "It would not explain Fausto's disappearance."

"So maybe Reggie killed Fausto, and died on his way back from moving the body," Liberty said grimly. "That's what we're looking for, right? Some evidence that Reggie killed this guy and hid his body?"

"Right." I was glad she'd said it so I didn't have to.

"Reggie crashed coming down the mountain," Liberty said. "He must've already hid the body farther up, or it would have been in the car. We won't find it at the crash site, assuming you're right."

That seemed like a pretty big assumption, but it was better than disbelief.

"I know. I'm not sure we'll find anything, and I have no idea what to do next if we don't." I swallowed past a lump in my throat. "I'm glad that you—" I couldn't say for sure that they believed me. "That you're going along with this. I don't know what else to do. I don't want to tell the whole world about my psychometry, and most people wouldn't believe me if I did."

No one said anything for a few minutes. We'd left the town behind and were heading toward some low mountains in the distance.

Macario shifted his focus to Liberty. "That thing you did with me. You also have some special power?" His tone was so neutral I couldn't tell if he was skeptical and trying to hide it, or if he had actually accepted meeting two women with strange powers so easily. Or maybe he felt like he was in a bizarre dream and was just going along with it.

"I see auras," Liberty said. "Colors or light surrounding people. I don't tell everyone about it either, but my friends know."

Was that a dig at me, because I hadn't said anything about my power last night?

"These are remarkable gifts," Macario said.

That jolted a laugh out of me. "More like a curse. It's never done me any good, but it's done a lot of harm."

That, unfortunately, got Macario's attention back on me. "If you see the truth, how is that harmful?"

"Well, I broke up my parents' marriage. I asked my dad who the pretty lady was he'd been hugging. I was five. I didn't understand that he was having an affair, but my mom did."

"That sounds like your father's fault, not yours," Liberty said.

I shrugged. "Maybe, but it was still miserable. I barely saw my father after that, and when I did, he wouldn't touch me. He didn't want me around his new wife and their kids either. When my mom figured out my so-called gift, she wanted me to check the men she dated. I had to find an excuse to touch their watch or wallet or something, and figure out what they were really like."

"That's terrible," Liberty said. "I'm not sure which of your parents I hate more."

"Thanks. I haven't seen either of them in a few years. When I was eleven, my mother remarried. I guess she decided she didn't want to know anything that might ruin her new marriage, so I went to live with my grandmother. That was okay. She pretended my psychometry didn't exist."

Macario muttered something in Spanish.

We turned onto a dirt road heading up the mountain. Trees grew close to the road, evergreens and something with lighter green leaves and pale bark. The green reminded me of home—my former home, in the Pacific Northwest. I wasn't sure how that made me feel.

Macario looked sad. "You know a little about my brother."

"Yes. I'm sorry, we're trying to find out what happened to him, and I'm making this about me."

"No, what I mean to say is, my brother is—or was—a criminal. A drug pusher, you would say. He made many bad choices. He grew up with love. We tried to give him a good life. Still he made his choices. It makes me sad, but it isn't because of me."

"I don't think your brother had empathy," I said. "I only got a quick glimpse, but I don't think he understood that other people have feelings. He didn't choose that, it was his brain chemistry or whatever. You couldn't have done anything to change him."

"Yes. But I still love him. That is how it is with families sometimes. We love them, and they hurt us."

I couldn't speak. I nodded to show I understood.

"I see why you don't tell people," Liberty said. "I won't tell anyone, you have my word. But I think if you decide you're ready to tell some of our friends in the future, it will be okay."

"Thanks." I had to clear my throat and take a moment to get myself under control. "It's hard making friends, because it seems unfair to learn things about them without their knowledge. But I can't say anything too quickly, or we never become friends in the first place, and how do I know if I can trust them to keep it secret?"

"It's not as bad for me," Liberty said. "Well, in my career

it was, but the Banditt Museum is more forgiving of eccentricities. But with friends, it was more annoying when they wanted me to entertain them."

"Yeah, I got some of that too, when I told a couple of girls in high school. I finally decided it's easier to keep it secret and keep to myself."

"Sorry to change the subject," Liberty said, "but why are we out here?"

"I want to find the place Reggie ran off the road. Maybe the wreck will tell us—me—something."

"Okay. I know it was about three miles up, but I don't know the exact spot. I assume we'll be able to see some signs, like broken branches."

I was glad for the excuse to stare out the window and focus on something else for a minute. Sharing my secret with Liberty and Macario had gone better than I'd dared to hope, but I still felt like I'd upended my entire life by revealing a truth I'd kept private for so long. And we hadn't even figured out how Fausto and Reggie had connected, what they had been doing that led to murder, or what happened to Fausto's body.

If we did figure it out, I might have to tell the world about the gift/curse/skill that got us this far. Or if not the world, at least the sheriff, and the whole town would probably know within a day. Somehow that felt worse than telling the world. In Seattle, people would forget fairly quickly, with so much else happening in the world around them. I could have hid in my apartment until it blew over, or at least until I ran out of money. In Bonneville, population 2000, I'd be branded a freak for life. Peyton would probably want to put me on display in the museum.

I felt bad for Macario, and I wanted to know what had happened, both to solve the puzzle and so I'd know if I was in danger. But I wasn't sure I could hope we'd find anything.

## Chapter Nineteen

"WE PASSED MILE marker two, half a mile back," Liberty said. "I'd guess Reggie ran off the road on his right, the downhill side—our left—but I don't know that for sure."

I hadn't noticed any mile markers, but I saw what she meant. Coming downhill, Reggie would be on the right side of the road from his perspective—or in the middle, as it wasn't very wide. He had a shallow ditch on his left, with a rocky slope up on the other side of the ditch. Running off the road on that side wouldn't be fun, but it probably wouldn't totally wreck the car. The heart attack might have killed him anyway, but I'd gotten the impression the crash itself had been bad. Hadn't someone said the tow truck struggled to retrieve the car? Victor? No, Peyton.

Then it hit me. The tow truck. The car wouldn't still be here. This was probably a fool's errand, and I was the head fool.

But we'd come this far, so I stared out the window as our car crawled along, Liberty driving about as slow as we could walk.

"Mile marker three," Macario said softly.

I glanced out the other window as we passed a small sign on a pole, with the number three against a green background.

"We'll turn around at the next mile marker if we don't find anything by then," Liberty said.

The minutes ticked by. Or maybe only a minute or two that felt much longer. Macario leaned forward and murmured something I didn't catch. Liberty slowed even more. She pulled over twenty feet on, just as I spotted the crumbled dirt at the edge of the road and the twisted branches with fresh breaks showing up pale and splintered.

We all sat in the car, staring at the area. I was glad I didn't see ghosts.

Macario looked at me. "You think you can learn something here?"

"I don't know. Probably not." I got out of the car anyway. There was just room for another car to pass, if needed. We hadn't seen anyone else out here yet.

We gathered at the edge of the road, looking down the slope. A car had definitely crashed here. They might have hauled out the car itself, but no one had bothered to clean up the bits of broken plastic and shattered glass. I shivered despite the sun beating on my head and shoulders. A few gnats buzzed around. The air smelled dusty and green, like vegetation baking in the sun, with a bitter smell that I hoped came from some roadside weeds.

"There's not much left to work with," Liberty said.

"I guess we should have tried to figure out where they took the wreck. Reggie probably had a lot of emotion in the last hours of his life. I might have been able to pick up something from the seat or the steering wheel." I shuddered at the thought of trying to find the car in some police lot or junkyard and reaching through the mangled mess to paw at the seat where Reggie had died. "Maybe not though."

Macario scrambled down the slope. He crouched, studying the scene. He shuffled over a few feet to squint at a dark stain on the dirt. "There is blood here, I think."

"That doesn't help us." Liberty looked at me. "You get readings from objects, right? Not from people, alive or dead."

I hesitated. I still wasn't sure why I'd even tried to get a reading from the carpet. Inspiration? Panic? It had been a faint hope, but it panned out. I hadn't felt anything from Fausto where his torso had lain, maybe because he was wearing clothing, or because some parts of the body transferred emotions better.

"I would have said yes, but . . . There's blood dried on the office carpet. That's how I figured out, or confirmed, who was the victim."

Liberty's eyebrows went up. "Huh. I wouldn't have expected a reading from blood."

"Me either," I said, "but it's not an exact science."

She gave a little huff of laughter.

"Okay, it's not any kind of science. And it's not like I've really tested all the limits and possibilities." Though maybe I should have. I'd spent most of my life trying to avoid using psychometry at all. This was the first time I really wished I knew how it worked.

Macario stood and brushed his hands on his jeans. "How does it work?"

"I don't know!" I winced at my own anger, which came out of frustration. "Sorry, I didn't mean to snap at you. I don't understand this any better than anyone else does."

He watched me steadily, calm and gentle despite the tragedy of our errand. I couldn't believe he was related to the psychopath who died in my office. (That's not an official diagnosis, obviously. But people who have no empathy were psychopaths, right? Or just assholes, but I thought Fausto was incapable of empathy, which sounded more like a mental illness.)

I also couldn't believe Macario had made me nervous the first time I saw him at the museum. On the other hand, he might have a gentle soul, but his intense focus was unnerving in its own way.

"How does it work in your experience?" he asked—gently, of course. "What is it like for you?"

"Well, I touch things, and I get these flashes—images, or sometimes phrases echoing in my head, or just emotion—or I don't get anything at all. I never know till I try." Or more likely, until it's forced upon me. "People must put out some kind of emotional energy, and that can leave a residue. If I touch an object that someone kept close for a long time, like jewelry they wore every day, I can tell some things about the person. Or if an emotion was very strong, especially if it was recent, that might override whatever else was there. That's the best I can explain it."

He frowned over this. "If you get what the person was feeling most recently, we need something Reggie Heap touched *after* he killed my brother."

I nodded. "I found the murder weapon, but that only told me what Reggie was feeling in that moment. The rock wasn't something he handled all the time, but I guess the intensity of the emotion was enough to leave an echo of the attack. I was hoping to find something that had picked up Reggie's emotions after that."

"But you got a reading from blood today?" Liberty asked.

"Yeah, but I don't know how the blood fits into it all. I don't normally touch bloody people."

Liberty snorted. "Good thing. Or maybe not, maybe you'd be able to identify illnesses that way."

"Please don't," I groaned. "The whole dilemma over whether I owe it to the world to use my *gifts*—" I said the word with heavy sarcasm "—to help other people . . ."

"You don't think you do?" Liberty asked.

"Do you go around telling strangers their auras are out of kilter?"

"It wouldn't do much good, since I can't tell them how

to fix it. But I see your point. I wasn't judging. I just wanted to know how you felt."

Macario had been watching this exchange, his eyes dark and solemn. "I cannot say what I would do in your place, and I am glad I do not have to make the choice. May we discuss the philosophy later? I am very grateful for your decision to help me."

I smiled at him. "But let's get on with the job? You're lucky that as much as I don't want to touch that blood, I have even less desire to hear about my responsibility to use my powers for the good of society."

"I didn't say that!" Liberty exclaimed. "Given your parents, I can see why you don't want people pestering you to find out whether their spouse is cheating."

"Or whether a boy likes them," I said. "I got that from the friends I told in high school. I almost wished they hadn't believed me. You do not want to know what goes through a teenage boy's head, or at least I didn't."

I studied the slope and found the spot that looked easiest to get down. I pictured stumbling and impaling myself on one of the broken branches jutting toward me. Good thing the dress code at the Banditt Museum was casual, so I was wearing sneakers rather than dress shoes.

As I edged down the slope, Macario moved below me and held out his hand. I took it, grateful for the physical support and even more grateful that he didn't act afraid of my touch.

The trees started about ten feet down, forming a sharp *V* with the slope, which was steep and covered with loose stones and pine needles. I had to duck under some of the remaining tree branches. I grabbed one for balance, but it bent so much it didn't really help. The whole setup was a disaster waiting to happen.

Hang on, the disaster had already happened. Good thing that was out of the way.

I dropped to my knees. I'd get dirty, but that was better than falling and getting tangled in tree branches, or worse. I tried touching a few of the broken plastic and glass pieces. No surprise that I didn't get any images. The steering wheel would have been the best bet, since Reggie must have gripped it as he drove up the mountain, thinking about what he'd done and what he was going to do. Maybe it would even show me what he saw when he pulled over to dump Fausto's body. It was probably too much to hope that I'd get a glimpse of a mile marker sign or an easily identifiable landmark, but maybe it would give us some direction.

But the bits that remained likely came from the outside of the car—windows, headlights, bumper. Unless Reggie spent a lot of time with his hand on the side window and I found some glass from that, I wouldn't get anything.

I was delaying. I knew it, and no doubt Liberty and Macario also knew or suspected it. They stood watching me, Liberty still on the road and Macario in the ditch with me. He stood about ten feet away, not hovering but alert. He seemed to have infinite patience, but his shoulders looked tense, and his fingers curled tightly where he'd hooked his thumbs into his belt loops.

"I don't want to get your hopes up," I said. "I don't normally get anything from people's skin. I assume it's because emotions change so often. Touching someone, I might feel a really strong emotion, but in that case, you usually don't need psychometry to tell what someone is feeling."

"I understand," he said.

I glared at the dark spot in the sand. I didn't relish touching someone's blood with my bare hands. Even medical professionals didn't do that. But the blood was now two weeks old, so it would be thoroughly dried out in the desert air and not likely to transmit disease . . . Right?

I also *really* didn't like the idea of getting images from Reggie's blood. I don't know why that sounded worse than touching something he'd owned—which was bad enough—but it *was* worse. Like I was reaching into his brain to pull out his memories.

Come to think of it, the blood on the office carpet had probably been from a head injury. Did that make a difference? Would I get less information if the blood came from someone's arm or chest or toe?

None of this made sense. The only way to know what would happen was to try it and find out. I'd dragged Liberty and Macario out here. It was time to do this, probably fail, and then we could go try something else. Unless they lost faith in me altogether.

I took some deep breaths, stretched and flexed my tight hands, fought against my instincts to pull back, and smacked my palm down on the spot of blood.

It felt like the blood slapped me back. Reggie was screaming, maybe not out loud but mentally, pain like fire exploding in his chest, shooting through his arm and jaw, the world blurring and then a moment of sharp focus as the car plunged forward, tree branches stabbing toward the window . . .

Someone was shouting.

I forced my eyes open. I was lying on my side, curled into a ball, dirt and pebbles or maybe broken glass pressing into the side of my face. Macario knelt behind me, murmuring in Spanish—comfort or prayers or maybe swearing—I couldn't understand the words, but they helped me focus on where I was now. He reached over me, gently took my wrist, and pulled my hand farther away from the blood. I curled my fingers over my palm and tucked my arm close to my chest.

Liberty skidded down the slope and knelt facing me, well back from the blood stain. "That was terrifying. Are you all right?"

"Yes." But I didn't try to move. I felt like I'd been battered by the car accident, everything aching and throbbing. I wouldn't have been surprised to find myself with broken bones.

They didn't speak again, waiting as I sorted through the images. Reggie's last moments shouted, but other thoughts had lurked behind that. He'd become a different person in the last weeks of his life. Someone he barely recognized. His pride and excitement and fear had locked in those thoughts, not quite erasing everything he'd been before, but washing over them, like trying to cover dark paint with something lighter. He'd needed another coat or two, another month or two, to complete his transformation.

Finally I uncurled and slowly sat up, queasy and groggy. Macario helped me with a hand on my back. When I was stable, he moved around to sit next to Liberty.

I tried to speak but it came out as a croak. I cleared my throat.

"Do you need water?" Liberty asked. "I have some in the trunk for emergencies. It will be warm though." Her lip curled as she looked at the bloodstain. "I have wet wipes and hand sanitizer too."

"Thanks," I managed. "How about some aspirin?"

She nodded. "The first aid kit should have three or four different painkillers. I'm sorry I ever suggested you try to read people's blood. Obviously that's a bad idea."

"Yes and no," I said. "I definitely don't want to do it on a regular basis. But I did learn something."

# Chapter Twenty

A TRUCK ROARED past on the road, barely slowing down to get by Liberty's car. A cloud of dust rolled over us. I closed my eyes and tried not to breathe. Someone coughed.

When the air cleared, Liberty said, "If there's nothing more for us here, let's get back to the car."

Fine with me. Liberty scrambled up the slope first. She stopped at the top and turned back as I got shakily to my feet. Macario stayed close as I made my way up the hill, and Liberty held out her hand. I'd invited her because I wasn't sure about Macario. I wanted somebody else along, and I figured Liberty was most likely to believe me. For once in my life, I'd gotten lucky, that these two people who'd never met each other were both on my side.

Unless they *had* met. Unless they were working together . . .

No, that was so unlikely as to be basically impossible. I shook off the thought and took Liberty's hand. She wasn't wearing jewelry. I got the impression of strength and confidence, but I don't know if any of that came from the psychometry or just from her firm grip as she helped me up.

I staggered to the car and leaned back against it. Liberty and Macario stood at the edge of the road, speaking softly. I tipped my head back and closed my eyes. I was hot but somehow also clammy, so the sun felt good on my face.

A *thunk* jolted me and I opened my eyes. Liberty had popped the trunk. She stepped around the back of the car and held out two bottles of water. Macario took one and I took the other with a shaking hand. I felt queasy and my whole body hurt, a headache pounding.

Liberty got her own water bottle, drank deeply, and wiped her mouth. "Now what?"

Macario looked at me. "My brother is dead."

I nodded. "I'm sorry."

He pushed a hand through his hair and down to the back of his neck. "I thought you might be playing some game. I didn't know what, so I went along to find out. But that—" He gestured toward the accident site. "I don't think that was fake."

I didn't say anything. *Thank you* would sound sarcastic. But in truth, his skepticism made sense, which ironically made me feel better.

"Do you know where the body is?" Liberty asked.

"Sort of. Reggie was very pleased with himself." I tried to think past the pain in my head and sort the feelings into a logical order. "They were up to something. Reggie and Fausto and at least one other person. Wait—" I looked at Macario. "Do you swear you didn't break into my house last night?"

"I did not." He frowned. "But someone did, so soon after . . ." He gestured toward the accident scene.

I nodded. "Two men. And if one of them was you, I won't press charges, but I'd really like to know how they fit into this, because I think they do."

Liberty scrunched up her face. "You're right, it can't be a coincidence."

"It wasn't me," Macario said. "I give you my word."

I took a deep breath and let it out slowly. "Okay. So Fausto was involved in something with someone here. I realize that's vague. All I know is it involved money, and they used the museum as a drop-off site."

"Drugs," Macario said. "It must be."

"That makes sense," Liberty said. "Fausto brought drugs from Mexico and met with somebody who would send them on to bigger markets in the US. But why bring the museum into it? Why not meet in the middle of nowhere?" She swung her arm in a gesture encompassing everything around us. "We have plenty of nowhere here."

"Fausto would think it funny," Macario said. "He liked to be clever, even when it was smarter to keep things simple. And if they left the drugs in the desert, wild animals might damage the packages. Anyone can come into the museum like a tourist. They wouldn't attract attention."

"Unless someone recognized Fausto from the WANTED poster, like I did. He probably didn't know it was posted in the sheriff's office."

"Even then, it wasn't much of a risk," Liberty said. "I'll bet most people don't pay any attention to those posters. I always assume the likelihood of seeing someone is so slim there's no point in studying them."

"Yeah." I wiped sweat from my forehead. "I wouldn't have noticed the poster if I hadn't already seen Fausto—I mean Macario, who looks enough like Fausto."

Macario leaned against the car next to me. "This starts to make some sense. But how did Reggie become a killer?"

I drank some more water as I thought through it. "He resented being used. Or really, he resented not being paid. He liked teen girls, and I think he lost other jobs over it. Fausto's group found out somehow and used that as blackmail."

Liberty made a huff of disgust. "I wish that surprised me more. So Reggie got drawn into this, and instead of figuring out how to get himself out and stop the criminals, he wanted his share?"

"More than his share," I said as the visions replayed in my mind. "He and Fausto argued. I don't think Reggie planned the murder, but he was angry and afraid. He grabbed one of the mineral samples on his shelf and hit Fausto. Then he drove here to hide Fausto's body, partly to avoid the murder charge, but also because he wanted to make it look like Fausto had disappeared with the money."

Liberty frowned. "What money?"

"The money from a drug delivery, I assume," I said.

"Right, but I didn't hear that they found money in Reggie's car. The police might keep some secrets if they were investigating all this, but they don't seem to be. Where is the money now?"

"I guess Reggie hid it before he dealt with the body." I had an idea about that, but it could wait. "That's probably why the men broke into my house, which used to be Reggie's house. The money is missing. Fausto is missing, and Reggie is dead. Either they don't believe Fausto ran off with the money, or they're not sure so they're hoping Reggie had it."

"And he did, but he'll never get to spend it." Liberty shook her head. "That's some karma right there."

"Reggie planned to stick around for a few weeks acting innocent. Then he'd quit his job, move away, and live off the money. Only . . ." I looked toward the place he'd died.

"Not a bad plan, except for the heart attack," Liberty said. "I didn't know he had it in him. Murder, that is. The heart attack is no surprise given his lifestyle."

"This is all interesting, but where is my brother?"

"In a culvert under the road," I said. "Reggie was bigger than Fausto but not especially strong. He couldn't move the body far, so he found a spot where there's a kind of sandy triangle beside the road—on the right side if you're going uphill. A big metal tube goes under the road, for water runoff, I'd guess. He managed to get the body in there."

It felt weird and wrong to keep talking about Fausto as *the body*, but I wasn't sure if it was better or worse to call him by name in the circumstances.

"There are probably a dozen or more culverts under this road," Liberty said. "Still, you really narrowed it down. And we know it's higher up the mountain than this."

"Probably not that much farther," I said. "Reggie was nervous and impatient."

We stood there another minute, sipping our water. No one seemed to want to take the next step. I didn't. Maybe they were still processing what I'd revealed.

Finally Liberty spoke. "Now what? It's been two weeks since all this happened. Macario, you don't want to see your brother like that. I know *I* don't."

I shuddered. It had been bad enough seeing the moments before Fausto died, and getting a glimpse of Reggie's view as he wrestled the body out of the car. I hadn't gotten as far as considering what kind of shape a body would be in after two weeks. We weren't in the heat of summer, but it had been warm. In the desert, would a corpse dry out, or—No, not thinking about it was definitely better.

"Also, how do we explain it?" Liberty went on. "No one will believe we just happened to stumble on it. Hikers do occasionally find bodies in the desert, and there might be some sign—or smell—we could claim drew us to it. But not Macario, that would be too much of a coincidence."

Macario rubbed his face. "You have done more than enough. Let us go back to town now. I will figure out how to retrieve Fausto."

Relief washed over me, leaving my legs weak. Maybe it was cowardly, but I didn't want to explain my gifts to anyone in law enforcement, and I *really* didn't want to see the body.

Liberty paced in front of us. "Maybe we could ask Elena—that's a friend of ours—to give her husband a tip. He's a sheriff's deputy. Or just call in an anonymous tip. Do people still do that? Can we even be anonymous anymore?"

My stomach growled loudly. I winced. "Sorry. I realize it's strange in the circumstances, but I'm famished. Doing this kind of thing takes a lot out of me."

"You say that like you uncover murders and find hidden bodies all the time. Okay, let's head back to town." But Liberty stepped closer to me and met my gaze. "By the way, your aura is gray."

"That sounds depressing."

"A pretty gray," she added. "Shiny, like that black stone . . ."

"Onyx?" I asked. "Or obsidian?"

"No, it has a silver sheen. You see it in gift shops a lot."

"Hematite?"

"That's the one."

That wasn't so bad. Hematite is pretty. I had no idea what it meant in terms of my aura, but I suppose it could be worse.

Macario straightened. "A car is coming."

Once Macario mentioned it, I recognized the engine

sound getting louder. We moved to the front of Liberty's car to make more room in the road.

A mostly black SUV came around a curve in the road. It had something attached to the front, an oversized bumper that looked like it could be used to push cattle out of the way—or maybe other cars, because as the SUV drew alongside us, I saw the star and word SHERIFF on the white doors. Sun glared on the windows so I couldn't see who was inside.

The vehicle stopped in front of us. The driver's door opened and Victor got out. He strolled toward us, one side of his mouth pulled up in a smile. "Fancy meeting you here. I got a call from someone who drove past a while ago. He noticed the stopped car and people off the side of the road. Thought I ought to check it out."

# Chapter Twenty-One

"WHAT ARE YOU up to?" Victor wore sunglasses so I couldn't tell if his gaze was on me or one of the others or shifting between us.

My mind felt like a slow-motion accident scene. I could see disaster coming but couldn't think of a single thing to say or do to prevent it.

Victor's mouth tightened. "Petra? Is everything all right?"

"Yes." I managed to get the word out but had absolutely no plausible explanation for why we were there. No reason we would be visiting the site of Reggie's accident that didn't involve psychometry and murder. I wanted to shout *I thought we'd have time to figure out a lie!*

Victor stepped forward, stiffening, his hand going to the gun at his side. "You!"

I turned. Liberty had her arms crossed, looking aloof and cool despite the heat that had me sweating—or maybe it wasn't the heat. Macario stood on the other side of the car, one hand on the roof above the passenger door. The impending accident was no longer in slow-mo—more like warp speed.

"No, that's not the guy, not the one from the WANTED poster," I said. "I was wrong about who I saw in the museum."

Uh-oh. Now I had to come up with an explanation for why I was out here with someone I'd met in the museum and thought I'd recognized on a WANTED poster. Someone who happened to be the wanted man's brother.

Victor's head turned slightly, as if he glanced at me before aiming back at Macario. "I'd like to check that for myself. Perhaps you'd care to come with me to the sheriff's office, sir."

"But—wait—" I had no idea what to say.

"It is fine. I will go with him." Macario came around the car with his hands held up to chest level, palms out.

"He has ID," I said.

"ID can be faked." Victor circled Macario and gave him a quick pat down. "Okay, get in."

Macario opened the back door of the SUV.

I took a jerky step toward him. "Can we do anything? A lawyer . . ." I wouldn't know where to find one or how to pay for one.

Macario glanced back at me. I couldn't read his expression. But then, I'd apparently missed most of what went on behind those sad eyes.

"He won't need a lawyer if he's not wanted," Victor said gruffly. "I just want to confirm he is who he says, find out what he's doing here, and any connection to the WANTED poster. He'll be out in a couple of hours, unless . . ."

With that vague but dire threat hanging, the two of them got in the vehicle. They pulled forward.

"Get in," Liberty said. "Let's get out of here."

"But . . ."

"I'll ask Elena to keep us updated on the situation."

"Oh. Right." I'd forgotten we had an inside woman at the sheriff's office. Handy.

I went around the car to the front passenger side. I felt stiff and awkward, as if I couldn't quite remember the video game codes to control my body. Once we were buckled in, Liberty headed uphill after the SUV.

"Where are we going?" I asked.

"To find someplace wide enough to turn around."

"Ah. Of course."

We went a few hundred yards. The sheriff's vehicle was out of sight around bends in the twisting road, but the dust hadn't settled behind it. Then we turned the corner and saw them up ahead, making a multi-point turn where the road widened a little. The SUV passed us going downhill, but I couldn't see past the glare on the windows.

Liberty turned at the same place. The hill on my side cut back into a *V*, leaving a sandy triangle between the road and the hill. The ground there was a couple of feet lower than the road. Liberty and I exchanged glances but didn't stop to see if a culvert ran under the road and if it held a body. One disaster at a time, please.

Finally Liberty spoke. “The good news is, Victor was so distracted by Macario looking like his brother that he forgot to pursue his question of what we were doing there.”

“Right. That feels a little like the frying pan, and now we’re in the fire. But I sure didn’t have an explanation.”

We passed the crash site again. It wasn’t obvious unless you paid close attention and spotted the broken branches or the debris scattered down the hill.

“Maybe he didn’t realize where we were exactly,” I said. “But he might figure it out later. I don’t know what to tell him.”

“You’re not required to tell him anything,” Liberty said.

How could I respond to that? Maybe I wasn’t legally required to explain myself, but I didn’t want to start my time in Bonneville with the sheriff as an enemy.

We came off the mountain and headed toward town in silence. Then Liberty made a sound between a sigh and a groan. “I’ll tell him I had a vision about the accident. That will explain what we were doing and help someone find the body.”

“But you don’t have visions. Do you?”

“No, but Victor thinks I’m a flake already. It won’t hurt my reputation with anyone who matters.”

I was torn between relief that I didn’t have to reveal my skill, guilt that I would let Liberty look like a fool so I didn’t have to, and suspicion because I couldn’t see what was in it for her.

"Why would you do that? We're not—" I wouldn't insult her by saying we weren't friends. She'd already been a better friend to me than many people I'd known much longer. "You barely know me."

She kept looking straight ahead, but I could see the scowl on her profile. "Maybe because I hate your family based on what you told me. You deserved better."

"Oh." I felt unmoored, floating somewhere above my body. My eyes stung.

"I can't fix the past, but I will not let Victor or anyone else drive you away because you have a talent most people can't understand."

I couldn't speak. I tried to get out the words *thank you* and only managed to whimper.

Liberty glanced over, her expression softening. "I know. It's okay."

It wasn't. Whatever it was, it wasn't *okay.* Some part of my mind still nagged at me to look for the angle, the way she could be manipulating me for her own benefit. Like the world would make more sense if I kept believing everyone was out for themselves. It felt safer keeping my head down at work and hiding away in my house with my animals in my free time. But at the same time, I felt like something inside me was breaking, or thawing, or maybe just starting to germinate, like a tiny green sprout pushing up through the ground, tender and vulnerable but maybe, possibly . . . ready to reach for the sun and grow.

"What now?" Liberty asked. "You need food."

"I think . . . I want to go home." I needed my animals.

She didn't say anything for five seconds. Then, "Home as in your house here, or are you running back to Seattle?"

"Here. There's no place for me to go in Seattle."

That seemed like it should be sad. I'd lived my whole life there, and it was no longer home. But I had no close friends. I barely spoke to my parents, and my grandmother had died three years ago. I'd given up my apartment, so if I returned, I'd have to go to a hotel. Seattle wasn't home. It was merely a place where I had lived.

Now *that* was sad.

I didn't want to go back to that, hiding in a place crowded enough that no one would notice me, pretending isolation suited me and I didn't need friends if I had pets. Granted, pets are objectively better than humans, but I still wanted both. I felt like an animal myself, a little mouse peeking its head out of its snug nest during the first spring thaw, wondering if winter was really over.

I wanted something different from my previous life, and I thought I might find it in this tiny New Mexico town.

But I still wanted to be alone with my pack now.

Liberty drove toward town. "If Victor calls, don't answer your phone. I'll find out from Elena what's happening, and whether we need to get Macario a lawyer after all, or if I need to go in there and explain that I dragged you two out to the crash site because of a vision. Don't say anything until we know what Macario told Victor, and what I had to tell him. You might want to take the afternoon off, in case he tries to find you at the museum, and don't answer the door."

"I can't take time off during my first week."

"Sure you can. Everyone knows about the break-in last night, so they'll assume you have to do something about that, or deal with other *new in town* stuff. That's assuming anyone even notices."

"I guess. So I shouldn't even tell them I'll be out?"

"You can, but you don't have to. If anyone wonders where you are, I'll say I was supposed to tell them you had to go home to deal with stuff, and I forgot. Or I'll be stuck at the sheriff's office all afternoon, and that will be my excuse."

I was leaving an awful lot to Liberty. I wasn't sure how I felt about that. Was this what friends did for each other? Would she expect favors in return? Did she have her own reasons for controlling the script? Was I being a bad friend with all these questions?

I wanted to be a good friend. I didn't want to be naïve and let people take advantage of me. It might take a while to find the balance.

We turned down the street toward my house. Something looked odd, a big white spot against the scene. I squinted, and we got closer, and I recognized the shipping container I'd packed with my stuff in Seattle. Well, I recognized *a* shipping container, and I assumed it was mine because it would be weird if it wasn't. Not that reality had presented any obstacles to weirdness yet this week.

Was my stuff supposed to arrive that day? What day was it? I felt like I'd been in town a month instead of less than a week. I fished out my phone and found that yes, I'd gotten an email about the delivery.

"There's your excuse," Liberty said as we pulled up to my house. "Although don't mention it unless you want people showing up to help you unload."

"Okay. Um." I ached from head to toe and wanted to sleep for a week. Surely I should be doing something, but I needed time to figure out what it was. "Thanks. For everything." It wasn't enough, but it was all I had at the moment.

Liberty gave me a wry smile. "We'll get through this. You've sure made life more interesting this week."

"Well, I like to make an impression." That was a lie, and a weak joke, and probably a foolish attempt at pretending to be almost normal. But Liberty's smile brought out the laugh lines at the corners of her eyes, as if she actually found me amusing.

I got out, paused for a moment with my hand on the car for stability, and decided I could make it into my house.

My house. *Mine.* Rented, but still.

I moved away from the car and waved as Liberty drove away.

"Petra!" Shelley was hobbling toward me from her porch, Toby at her side. I stepped closer to the fence and grabbed it for balance as they came panting up.

"Can you believe it?" Shelley asked. "My storage shed was broken into!"

"What? I thought Dennis didn't see any signs of a break-in."

"That's what he said. But I went out there a minute ago. The lock was cut." She looked sheepish. "I can't tell if anything was stolen. It's a little cluttered."

"Huh. Do you think Dennis . . ." He'd have to be pretty bad at his job not to notice a cut lock.

"He wouldn't need to cut the lock. He had my key."

That wasn't what I'd been thinking. "Um, you don't think Dennis had anything to do with the break-in, do you?"

"Oh, no, there's not a chance in a blue moon, really. He got in some trouble when he was younger, but he settled down when Elena got pregnant and they married."

"Anyway, if he wanted to come back later to finish a search, he could have left it unlocked. So . . ." Wow, my mind was chugging along at the speed of a sedated sloth. "Did someone come back and break in after Dennis checked the shed, or did Dennis not realize they broke into the shed last night?"

Shelley frowned over that. Toby panted and slobbered. "They wouldn't come back after being chased away. Would they?" (That was Shelley, not Toby, in case there was any confusion.)

"I don't know what they would do. I don't understand any of this."

"Maybe I'll call the police this time." Instead of the sheriff's office where Dennis worked, she must mean. Did Shelley not trust Dennis after all?

"Have you thought of anything else about the people you saw last night? Could you tell if they were tall or short or one of each?"

"It's hard to judge from a distance . . . Wait, I saw them come out your door. They seemed large, or tall anyway, against the doorway. I saw Reggie come out often enough, and he was no bean pile, but he was taller than I am." Even with my mind not working well I could figure out she meant *beanpole*, not *pile*.

"Both tall then." That supported Macario's claim that he wasn't one of them.

She nodded. "They wore dark clothing, and I couldn't see their faces because of the ball caps. That's about it. No one had an obvious limp or anything like that." She chuckled. "If they did, I'd have to suspect myself."

Toby gave a snuffling *woof* and grumbled.

"He's probably telling us he knows exactly who the intruders were based on their smell." Shelley looked down at her dog fondly. "It must be annoying that humans miss such obvious clues and don't even listen when you explain. Oh, your stuff arrived." She gestured toward the storage container.

I stopped myself from answering *No kidding?* or *Yes, I had noticed.* Apparently I could still be snarky even when exhausted. Good thing I had so much practice keeping my thoughts to myself.

"I hope it's not in your way. It might take me a few days to unpack everything."

"No, it's fine. Good thing you're the last house on the street. I'm all discomfitulated."

What now? Oh, she must have combined discomfited and discombobulated or similar words.

"Anything I can do?" I desperately hoped the answer was *No.*

"I guess not. Thanks. You look wiped out, and no wonder after last night. I'll bet you didn't sleep a wink."

I didn't disabuse her of the notion. "I was heading in to take a nap."

Shelley seemed like the kind of person who would respect a nap. Toby, too, for that matter.

"You do that. Good gracias, Petra, you've had a poor introduction to our town. I promise it's not like this *all* the time."

I hoped it wasn't like this *any* of the time.

"Oh, I've been meaning to ask. I found Reggie's laptop computer in a cupboard above the refrigerator." No point keeping that a secret, since it was probably all over town. "I didn't find the charging cord though. Did you come across it when you were clearing out his stuff?"

"Well, to tell the truth, I had somebody else do that. I can't get down on the floor anymore. I hired a couple of local housecleaners, and they brought me the boxes of Reggie's stuff. I think there were several cords, all bundled together in a box."

One more mystery solved. Why had I wasted so much time worrying about the power cord? I'd know a lot more about prioritizing and following clues by the time this was all over—assuming it ever was. Not that I ever expected or wanted to use these skills in the future.

I patted Toby on the head, said goodbye, and headed to my house. But not to nap. I had to think. I'd learned a lot in the last few hours. What did it all mean? I no longer had to worry about Reggie's murderer, since *he* was the murderer. But his death and Fausto's hadn't put an end to whatever was happening. The break-in last night and the return to check Shelley's shed proved that.

I needed to make sense of it all before someone else got hurt.

# Chapter Twenty-Two

FIRST I GOT my animal fix. Wulfenite and Xanthitane, the guinea pigs, squeaked in delight when I entered and groomed my fingers. Then Gypsum, one of the white rats, crawled onto my shoulder and snuffled under my hair. I felt better after that.

I heated soup and ate on the couch. Amber rubbed against my shin a few times, while Jet claimed my lap to ensure I wouldn't get too comfortable while trying to eat. One must keep one's servants in line.

I talked to the cats in between bites of soup. "I liked Dennis and Elena, and they have four kids. Granted that's a reason to want more money, but I don't want Dennis to be guilty of anything."

Amber looked up at me. "Merrp."

"Yeah, what I want doesn't matter. I have to get past that and figure out whether he *is* guilty of something. It doesn't make sense that he would say the storage shed wasn't broken into and then come back later to break into it. He had a perfect chance to claim the thieves had already gotten in there. He could have searched it himself last night in the guise of looking for clues."

Jet twisted and flung out one paw, bumping my hand.

"Yeah, I can't believe I said *the guise of looking for clues* either. But somebody is looking for something connected to Reggie. They might not know Fausto is dead, but they'd know the money disappeared, so they must be looking for it—or drugs, but Reggie was excited about money. Could be both though. Maybe Fausto brought the drugs and was ready to take the money. Reggie might not know what to do with drugs, but the criminals would still want them."

Amber hopped up on the couch next to me and settled down in a loaf. Jet yawned and stretched.

"Oh, am I boring you? So sorry."

It was hard to imagine cheerful Elena married to a criminal. Of course, she wouldn't be the first woman to discover that her husband had a secret life. But it was also hard to imagine Dennis helpfully taking the time to secure my windows while desperate to find missing drug money. It did give him a chance to go through my house on his own, but he was pretty quick about it, and he'd already been through the house with Gonzales.

"Oh! I'm an idiot."

Jet purred.

"We got chairs out of the shed last night." It had been dark, and I'd been thinking about spiders and scorpions, but I remembered waiting while Shelley unlocked the shed, so the lock hadn't been cut then. She must have been too flustered to remember that.

Dennis and Gonzales had learned that Shelley stored some of Reggie's things in her shed. They must have filed reports on my break-in, so everyone at the police station and sheriff's office would know by morning, and I'd already learned how fast news spread. Would the reports state that Shelley said she'd stored some of Reggie's things in there? That seemed less likely, since as far as they should know it wasn't relevant, but one of the guys might have mentioned it to his colleagues.

Two people broke in. Shelley called the police. Elena called her husband, who probably reported it to the sheriff's office on his way there. The two men ran away from my house before we or the police arrived. Had they finished searching and happened to run away just in time? Surely not, since the thieves returned to search Shelley's storage shed. They hadn't finished the job, and they ran away before they could have heard the sirens. The intruders might have a police scanner—or they might work for the police or sheriff's office or have a contact there who'd warned them.

If one or both of the thieves worked at one of those places, it would explain why they had returned to search the storage shed. They might not have thought about the shed until Dennis and Officer Gonzalez turned in their reports.

It kept coming back to the police or sheriff. Dennis could have decided he didn't have time to search thoroughly then, so he came back later. But it just didn't seem likely.

The shed was crammed full of stuff, but most of it was covered in dust. It should have been pretty easy to figure out what had been put in there recently, so it wouldn't take long to search. Unless they thought Shelley knew about the money and was intentionally hiding it—but no one had tried to get into her house, and I wasn't convinced Toby was that much of a guard dog. He might protect Shelley, but as long as she wasn't in danger, he seemed friendly, and he knew Dennis.

Plus the intruders had run away, and when we drove up not five minutes later, Dennis's police cruiser was already there. It was asking a lot for him to run back to where his car was hidden and drive up again. And finally—I might actually be getting the hang of this analysis stuff—he was wearing a sheriff's uniform. He could have pulled off the ball cap he wore while breaking in, and Shelley might not have noticed the uniform in the dark, but surely Dennis wouldn't want to risk anyone identifying his uniform while he was committing a crime.

"He'd have to be diabolically clever and coolheaded to commit a crime while on duty in uniform so he could pretend to show up minutes later and investigate," I said aloud. "I can't see it of Dennis, and frankly, anyone that clever wouldn't involve Reggie in his schemes."

So Dennis probably wasn't involved. But the law enforcement connection might still hold. It was a disgusting abuse of power, but they probably had the knowledge and connections to run a drug ring. I didn't know any local law enforcement besides Dennis, Officer Gonzales, and Victor, but there must be other officers.

And Victor . . . When I first visited Victor, I'd mentioned Reggie's missing keys. He'd returned them after that but hadn't said anything at the time. Surely he wouldn't have forgotten he had them. Bonneville wasn't such a hotbed of crime that he'd be juggling multiple cases.

Victor had known I'd be at book club when the break-in happened. When Elena called her husband, Dennis probably alerted the sheriff, or maybe Victor had been monitoring police channels already. He'd know he had to get out quickly.

Wait a minute . . . If Victor and Fausto were running drugs together, Victor knew Fausto. Yet he'd seemed startled and alarmed to see Macario. Did he know who Macario was? Macario said he'd talked to the police about his brother. Maybe the police hadn't told the sheriff's office—but surely they would share that kind of info. Maybe Victor panicked at the sight of Fausto's brother with us and wanted to separate us. Or he might have thought, at first glance, that Macario was Fausto. Then he'd wonder why we were with Fausto and what the man had been doing in the two weeks since the money disappeared. Once he realized his mistake, he might cover his reaction by taking in Macario for questioning, which also made a good excuse to take in Macario and interrogate him about his brother's drug deals.

Add in Liberty's discomfort with Victor's aura. She hadn't been sure it meant anything, but her instincts told her to keep away, and I thought she had the good instincts.

Victor had visited me at the museum. I'd tried to interpret his unexpected friendliness as small town life, or interest in the first youngish female to move there in a while. But he'd been intrigued by the locked safe.

If I were Reggie, and I had a lot of money I wasn't supposed to have, the safe would seem like a good place for it. Maybe they'd used it in the scheme as a place to leave the drugs and the money for the exchange. That could explain why Reggie was involved in the first place. Maybe his job had been to unlock and lock the safe as the drugs and money came and went. That way Victor wouldn't risk being seen with drug runners, and Reggie must've seemed too pathetic to go against orders. Now, even if Victor knew or suspected the money was in the safe, he wouldn't be able to get into the safe without the combination, and it was too heavy to move to a location where they could spend time working on it unobserved. Could one change the combination on those old safes? The thieves might be searching for the combination written down somewhere, or hoping to find the money if Reggie had already removed it from the safe. I'd finished the soup but was still hungry. I nudged Jet off my lap. I could feel his glare on my back as I headed to the kitchen to make a sandwich.

Was Victor one of the two men who'd run away from

my house last night? I'd been trying to ignore the thought that strangers had been pawing through my things (what little I had). It was worse when it wasn't a stranger. It was too easy to picture Victor walking through the house, studying the rooms with their minimal belongings, judging them. Judging me.

No, he wouldn't bother thinking about me. He wanted the money.

I looked up at Onyx, who was watching me spread mustard on bread. "I can't believe I'm worrying about *Mexican drug lords*. Or is it a cartel? Either way, I don't want their attention. But maybe this wasn't that big. Maybe Fausto had a little business of his own. We can hope, right?"

Onyx chirped his agreement.

I leaned on the counter and closed my eyes for a moment. Had I just convinced myself Victor was part of a drug ring? Everything seemed to fit. Maybe other answers fit as well though. It's not like I knew everyone in town. But with Reggie's involvement, the museum seemed to be a key, and I'd met almost everyone who spent much time there. Was the drug ring just Reggie, Fausto, Victor, and an unknown tall man who broke in with Victor? Or was someone else at the museum involved? If neither of their intruders had a beard, that left out Kit and Peyton, and surely the criminals wouldn't trust a teenager like Austin. Gloria and Haven could not be mistaken for tall men. Liberty might be, but she'd been at book club.

She'd also gotten me away from my house that night. Intentionally, so people could search it? Liberty had been a good friend, as far as I could judge, but my knowledge of good friends was mainly through TV shows. Was she part of all this, befriending me so she could keep an eye on my activities, in case I found Reggie's money or a clue to it? Were she and Victor faking their mutual dislike? Had she volunteered to tell Victor she'd had the vision as an excuse to meet with him and tell him everything?

It didn't feel right. I didn't want it to be true. But maybe I was fooling myself, desperate to hold on to the belief that someone had liked me and cared what happened to me.

I didn't like doubting her, but I needed to know whom I could trust. Maybe I could use the safe to set a trap for Victor, but first I needed to know who was really on my side.

Good thing I had a way of seeing past what people chose to share, and access to a vast array of things that Liberty had handled.

"Psychometry got me into this," I told Onyx. "Maybe it can get me out again."

So much for my afternoon off. I drove back to the museum.

When I entered the museum, at least a dozen people were browsing the gift shop, paying their entrance fee, or otherwise milling around. A tour group gathered around Kit, Gloria worked the cash register, and Peyton was explaining the museum map to someone. I wove through the customers and slipped down the hallway to the break room, which was empty. Luck was with me, but I probably shouldn't get used to it.

My first thought had been to visit sections of the museum and try to read items from the displays, but that was problematic. I wouldn't know for sure who had put up most displays, since some had been there for decades. Also, while the museum curators must have handled the artifacts briefly, that wouldn't typically override whatever was left behind by the people who previously had the objects. Finally, I'd feel too weird going to the alien diorama and asking the aliens for information on Liberty.

But hadn't she said each of them had their favorite coffee mug? And those got washed and set in the dish rack! Now all I had to do was remember which mug each person had. Oh, and get through the test without my coworkers wandering in and wondering why I was fondling their coffee mugs.

I didn't need to check Peyton's mug, since I'd already read his watch. I started with Kit. He'd left the gate unlocked, which could have been laziness but might have been an attempt to allow someone else in—but who? Fausto, if he didn't know if Fausto was dead?

According to his coffee mug (and I realize how odd that sounds), Kit was a bit of a man child. He resented that Peyton wasn't willing to hand over control of the museum, but at the same time Kit was fairly lazy and didn't want to do the work that would be required to run the place. He'd be happier if he could accept that he enjoyed giving tours and didn't actually want the responsibility of running a business, but someone had been poisoning his thoughts, telling him he deserved more. Another relative? I wasn't sure, but in any case, I didn't sense that he was involved with drugs or murder.

Liberty and Haven . . . I'll respect their privacy and just say I got interesting readings but nothing that connected them to a drug smuggling operation.

That wasn't the most exciting part of my day, but by the time I left, my heart was racing, my hands stung, and I was trembling with relief that none of my coworkers were (probably) murderers.

And my luck held, since no one interrupted me.

I headed back to the geology wing thinking about the people I thought I could trust: Liberty, Shelley, Peyton, Macario. Probably Mrs. Banditt and Haven, Elena and Dennis, and the women I'd met the night before. Kit, but only to a certain extent.

People I couldn't trust: Victor. But who was the second intruder? Officer Gonzalez? Was the rivalry between the police and sheriff's office a cover? But all the reasons Dennis didn't fit as one of the intruders applied to Gonzales as well, plus he'd heard Shelley say she'd put some of Reggie's things in the shed. That would've been a great opportunity for him to search the shed, but he'd sent Dennis to do it instead. So probably not Gonzalez. That would be a relief if I had to call the police on the sheriff.

My ratio of decent people/possible friends to villains was actually fairly good.

I'd been passing tourists without paying much attention, but when I entered the rocks and minerals wing and saw people, I jerked to a stop. A woman squatted next to a child, peering into a case of pretty mineral samples. The man standing nearby glanced at me. I forced myself to smile and keep moving. This was not, in fact, my private sanctuary. Darn it.

In my office, I shuffled some papers around so it might look like I was working. Really I was debating how to prove what I thought I knew. Reggie had killed Fausto, and Reggie was beyond the law now, but Macario would want to retrieve Fausto's body for burial. And somehow we needed to expose the drug ring and prove the sheriff was part of it.

I might be able to lure Victor into revealing himself. He'd noticed the old safe and wanted to see it opened, so quite possibly Victor thought Reggie had hidden the money there. (I thought so too. We were running out of other options.) What if I told Victor I'd found the combo and asked if he wanted to see me open the safe?

He might simply confiscate whatever was in the safe and claim he was going to investigate it, as sheriff. But if he guessed I knew even a quarter of what I did know, he wouldn't want me as a witness. Also, it would be hard to prove Victor had anything to do with the drug ring unless I got him to admit something, maybe on a recording. Then he'd definitely want to stop me.

I wasn't loving this plan.

I checked the museum catalog number on the safe and started looking through the files. It might be hard to get Victor to admit anything if I invited him to see the opening of the safe but couldn't actually open it.

I needed to come up with a plan that had a higher chance of catching the bad guys than of killing me. Much higher, ideally. I'd also need backup. But I'd look for the combination while I pondered.

You might expect a filing system based on artifact numbers to be, you know, numerical. Or not, if you've been paying attention to anything that could loosely be called a system at the Banditt Museum. It took about an hour before I figured out how the files should have been set up. *Should have been* based on the system some madman had devised, that is. We hadn't gotten close to *should have been* by any rational standards. And about a third of the files didn't even follow that eccentric system, so either other people had failed to understand it since the original madman, or they just didn't care. But at least things were starting to make . . . not sense, but like when you get to the stage of a sudoku where you can believe all the numbers will add up, even if you can't figure out how yet.

I took a break and checked my phone for messages. Nothing important. Where were Liberty and Macario? What had they told Victor?

I dictated a text to Liberty, careful to make the message vague on the off chance the sheriff could see it: *I have some ideas about the project we previously discussed. Find me at the museum or let me know when you have time to plan it.*

I set my phone on the desk so I'd quickly hear and see any replies. I hoped the sheriff wasn't giving Macario too hard a time.

I watched the next group of tourists that came in. It was helpful to know what caught their attention, so I was working, right?

They liked large, colorful mineral samples. Ooh, big surprise, great market research.

I went back to the files. An hour later, I found the safe combination. I was more surprised than excited. Why hadn't Reggie removed it from the files? Maybe he'd assumed the filing system was enough of a maze to deter anyone looking for it, or he'd found the combination somewhere else and didn't even know it was in the files.

I stretched and rolled my shoulders. I'd forgotten to refill my water bottle, so I hadn't had anything to drink in hours, which alone could explain the headache and dry throat. Looking through file cabinet drawers hadn't eased the stiffness from my horrible psychic vision either.

Still no messages. I'd check the safe and head to the workroom to fill my water bottle at the sink. A glance through the door glass showed the geology hall blessedly free of tourists. This close to closing, it would probably stay that way.

I stepped out into the main room. Something moved to my right. I jumped and gasped. So did the man in the corner of the room.

"Oh, you startled me." He laughed. "I didn't realize anyone was in there."

I gulped as my racing heart debated whether it was safe to slow down. "We're even. I didn't realize anyone was in the room."

He glanced toward the far door. "Yeah, I just wanted a few minutes alone while my wife and kids take pictures with the outlaws and aliens." He blew out of breath. "Long road trip. I needed some quiet. Er, your room here is interesting too. Nice rocks and . . . stuff."

I scrambled for something to say. "Maybe I should get rid of some displays and put in a lounge for exhausted road trippers. I'd be the most popular stop in the museum." Sadly, that's what it would probably take.

He grinned. "Add a bar and I promise I'll stop on the way back. Well, I should be going."

"I didn't mean to drive you away." I wanted him gone, but I couldn't show it.

He glanced at his watch. "No, I need to collect them and figure out a place for dinner. Any suggestions?"

"Well, I hear the diner is good but I haven't actually eaten there since I'm new in town."

"Oh. Well . . ." We looked at each other awkwardly for a moment before he said, "Good luck with it. Bye." He headed toward the far door.

Whew. Guess I was a little jumpy, though not without reason. Once I dealt with the current garbage, I'd stop panicking at the slightest surprise. Probably. I hoped.

Once the man was gone, I knelt in front of the safe. I had the numbers, but no instructions about turning the dial all the way around before the next number or going directly to it or whatever. I tried a couple of things before finally the handle turned.

The money, or anything else I might find, wasn't mine. I literally didn't want to touch it. Yet I still got a buzz of excitement. This must be how prospectors felt when they found a gold seam. My hard work had paid off. (Yes, I'm making a parallel between going through file cabinets and the backbreaking work of mining. Seriously, you should see those files.)

I pulled open the safe door to reveal an off-white satchel. I couldn't see inside it and wouldn't check it without gloves, but I stared for a while. Fausto had died over this. Reggie too, in a way. And *I'd* found it—me, not law enforcement trying to stop drug running or any of the villains who wanted it.

"Well, what do we have here?" The familiar voice came from behind me.

My vision blurred until I remembered to breathe. I slowly turned to see Victor—No, *the sheriff.* I needed to think of him like that so I'd remember he wasn't a friend, or even a friendly acquaintance.

He looked down at me with hard eyes and a harder smile, his hand on the gun at his side.

## Chapter Twenty-Three

SHOULD I SCREAM? Play innocent and pretend I was happy to see Victor? I didn't think I could act that well.

A faint *thunk* came from the far end of the room. I looked past the sheriff. The man I'd startled, and who had startled me, stood just inside the door. I wasn't alone with the sheriff after all!

The moment of hope died as I noted the door he'd closed.

"The mysterious second man." The words sounded like they were coming from far away instead of from my own lips. "You were keeping an eye on me." No point in denying my knowledge now.

"I knew you had to be involved," Victor said. "I still don't understand how, but nothing else makes sense."

"Would you believe it's sheer accident?" I asked.

He shrugged. "I guess it doesn't matter now. Grab that bag."

I looked at the satchel in the safe. "No."

"What?" He loomed over me. "Give it to me."

I shifted away from the safe. "Get it yourself." Maybe it

wasn't the best idea to antagonize him, but we were already about as antagonistic as we could get. I might as well save myself the discomfort of touching a satchel that Fausto and Reggie had probably both handled.

He glared at me for a few seconds. Then he glanced at the other man. "Get the cameras."

"I'm sorry, cameras?" I demanded.

Victor smirked. "Like you said, we've been keeping an eye on you. After what happened with Reggie, I wasn't taking any more chances."

The second man went over to the tall shelves, reached up to the top, and stuck something in his pocket. He crossed the room and did the same on that side. The cases were too tall for me to have seen anything sitting on them, and these cameras were tiny, easy to overlook. So the good news: If the cameras recorded and weren't only used for live monitoring, then they'd recorded these men finding me in the room. They might even have voice recordings.

The bad news: Unless I could find a way to escape, taking the cameras with me, no one would ever know about the recordings.

I carefully did not look at the exit door ten feet away. It would let me out behind the museum, but then what? The yard would almost certainly be empty, so no help and no witnesses. I wasn't adjusted to the altitude, I couldn't outrun even one fit man, let alone two.

Forget the cameras. I'd have a hard enough time saving

myself.

I needed to distract, delay, or destroy Victor and the other guy. I pushed to my feet, a little wobbly, and looked at the new player. "I'm sorry, we haven't been formally introduced."

He studied me. "I don't get it. Nothing in your background says you should be involved in something like this. So is this your first attempt at crime, or have you just never been caught before?"

I glared at Victor. "You did do a background check on me."

"Well, one of us did," mystery man said. Maybe he worked in the sheriff's office too.

"Shut up, both of you," Victor said. "Out of the way."

Nothing would please me more than getting *far* out of the way. Some naïve part of me had been holding onto a sliver of hope that Victor was a good guy, that he might try to arrest me because he thought I was one of the criminals, but he'd ultimately help. That hope had just died. Whatever he had planned now would be far less pleasant than arrest.

I backed away from the safe slowly, dizzy, keeping the old mining cart between me and Jerk. Yeah, you don't give me your name, I get to call you whatever I want.

*The mining cart.* It was heavy and wasn't fastened to the tracks. But it was heavy and would only move in the direction the tracks pointed. I'd hardly save myself by grunting and slowly pushing the metal cart off the tracks with the men standing back and watching. To use the cart as a weapon, I'd have to get at least one of them in the right place. And hope the other cared more about helping his colleague than chasing me. That didn't seem like a bet with good odds.

Victor squatted in front of the safe with the bag between his knees. I needed him to back up three feet, and if Jerk would move forward about five feet, so they stood close enough together to hug each other, I could take them both out at once, as long as the mining cart moved quickly enough that they couldn't dodge it.

Those odds were not improving.

I looked at Jerk and whispered, "I think he knows about us."

"What?"

"There's no point in pretending." I had no idea where I was going with this. I was so lightheaded the room seemed to shift with gray spots and sparkles. I didn't think I was visibly shaking, but I couldn't say for sure.

Victor stood and turned toward us, scowling. "What is she talking about?"

"I have no idea. I never spoke to her before today." Jerk moved toward Victor and they both turned, not quite shoulder to shoulder but clearly them versus me.

"I'm just saying . . ." I stumbled and grabbed the edge of the mining cart. I wasn't faking it. It felt like my mind was floating outside my body, sending panicked commands that contradicted each other.

They were too far away. If I pushed the cart now, it would roll right past them, or maybe clip Jerk's foot if he didn't step aside in time. I shifted around to the end of the cart opposite them and leaned both my hands on it as if I was settling it for a long conversation.

"Come on," I said, wishing I knew Jerk's name. "It's time to choose."

He gave a huff of laughter. "She's crazy."

"I wouldn't be surprised," Victor said. "She hangs out with Liberty."

Jerk glanced down at the bag Victor held. "Is that it? It's all there?"

"I'm not going to count it now," Victor snapped. "Let's get out of here."

"What about her?"

They both looked at me. They weren't in a great position, but in a moment they'd come around the mine cart to grab me, which would make their position—and mine—even worse. Now or never, fortune favors the brave, and all those clichés.

I bent my knees and pushed the mine cart toward them with all the force I could manage.

It shrieked with that metal on metal sound that made eardrums throb. For a moment it felt like everything was moving in slow motion. Then the front wheels dropped off the end of the tracks, and the cart bounced forward. I fell to my knees as the weight shot away from my hands.

The men swore and jumped away. The cart hadn't come close to hitting them, but it had distracted them for a moment. I scrambled up and ran for the back door.

I shot out into the yard. But now what? I couldn't lock the door behind me. I didn't have the workroom key on me. I didn't have a phone to call for help. (Note to self: Start carrying phone at all times! Also, figure out the entire plan before initiating the first part.)

The gate beckoned, but it might take precious seconds to open the combination lock and lock it again to delay them.

The door behind me was already opening. I darted alongside the building. Where could I go? I didn't have keys to any other back doors. The building didn't have windows, so I couldn't look for people inside and rap to get their attention. I hadn't explored the yard thoroughly, but I assumed it was enclosed by the chain-link fence with its razor wire top. I'd merely traded one prison for another.

"Stop!"

I kept running as I glanced over my shoulder. Victor had his gun out. Surely he wouldn't shoot. Or would he get rid of me and claim I was resisting arrest?

My foot caught on something and launched me forward. I landed flat out.

Someone laughed. I scrambled up, trying to get air in my lungs, coughing on the dust cloud my fall had raised.

"Come on, Petra, don't make a fuss," Victor said. "How do you think this is going to end?"

Not in any way I wanted. I stumbled to a piece of old farm equipment. My farming knowledge was lacking and I didn't have time to study the machinery to determine its purpose. I just cared that it put a lot of metal between me and Victor's gun.

If it had only been him, maybe I could keep circling it opposite him and hope if he shot, the bullets wouldn't get through the metal. But with two of them . . .

I was trapped. I looked wildly around the yard but no miraculous escape route appeared.

At least the cameras back there would provide a record of my death or kidnapping. If anyone bothered to look. If Victor didn't get to them first.

Victor whispered something to the other man, who nodded. Victor stayed where he was but Jerk veered off, starting a wide circle around me.

"There are cameras!" I shouted. "They're watching right now!"

Jerk stopped and looked back at Victor. Maybe I'd just warned the sheriff that he needed to confiscate those recordings before anyone else saw them, but I'd rather stay alive than prove how I'd died.

Victor muttered something and looked back at the building. I took advantage of their hesitation to scan for anything that might help me escape or fight back. Nothing. Nothing at all.

"We just want to talk to you," Victor said.

I finally spotted something useful—a metal bar a couple of feet long laying on the ground. But I'd have to step away from my protective farm equipment to reach it.

Victor kept talking loudly. "Maybe you'll lose your job when everyone finds out you're involved with drug running, but if you testify against your partners, you'll get off pretty easy."

Oh, so now he was trying to control the narrative in case the cameras were recording sound. Or else he was offering me a deal—pretend I was the drug runner, and they wouldn't kill me, at least not until later.

"I had nothing to do with it," I shouted. "Reggie killed Fausto and left me with the mess."

"*Reggie* killed—" Victor broke off.

I lowered my voice so Victor and Jerk could hear but maybe the cameras wouldn't. "Yeah, your pet geologist decided he'd rather take the money than follow your orders. So maybe you should think twice before messing with another one."

Pretty sure I was not making a convincing case, but every second I delayed them was a second where I might come up with a better plan.

"So you knew Reggie. That's how you—" Victor broke off, maybe remembering that this might be recorded. When he spoke again, he projected his voice. "You were part of the drug ring I've been chasing all along. Guess I should check your shipping container. Could be some interesting things in there."

What to say? Deny knowing Reggie? Would it make a difference if I convinced Victor and Jerk that I was an innocent bystander? Should I challenge Victor's claim since there was a slight chance somebody besides him might check the video later and hear this?

Jerk was sidling sideways, trying to get around behind me while I was distracted by Victor. I'd had enough of talking anyway.

I darted out, ducked down to grab the metal bar, and came up swinging. Jerk flinched back and I stumbled on the uneven ground. The metal bar hit him on the hip, which was not where I'd aimed, if you could call any part of my wild flailing *aiming*. He yelped and fell to his knees.

I caught my balance, using the metal bar like a cane, and glanced at Victor. He had his gun out. I scrambled behind the next large thing in the yard, the old car Macario said he'd slept in. I crouched behind a wheel. Bullets could go through cars though, right? This seemed less safe than the farm equipment, but it put me a little closer to the gate out of there. Unfortunately, I'd dropped the metal bar in my panic.

"Resisting arrest?" Victor said. "You're just making things worse."

"For all your threats, you have yet to claim you're arresting me," I yelled.

Jerk groaned and muttered something. I peeked over the trunk for a second. Jerk was standing, and Victor joined him.

They spoke in low voices.

I ran toward the next thing that offered any protection and was in the direction of the gate, a piece of old mining equipment with metal gears three feet across mounted on a heavy, rusted base. The thick metal would stop a bullet better than the car, but the odd shape offered less coverage than the original farm equipment.

I gasped for air, gearing up to make another run. The gate was thirty feet away and I'd need time to get through it. *Kit, I hope you were the last one through and you were too lazy to turn the dials.*

Jerk limped past the opposite side of the mining equipment, while Victor circled around toward me. In a second, he'd have a clear shot. I'd be exposed the whole way to the gate. I'd never make it in time.

"Petra!" The shout came from the building.

Victor froze. For a second I froze too, before swinging toward the building to see Liberty in the open door to the geology wing, waving her arm to urge me toward her.

I didn't have time to think, so I just ran. Around the mining equipment so Victor no longer had a clear shot. Past Jerk, as he looked around for the source of the yell. Liberty stepped back and I darted past her.

I'd made it inside! Breathless and stumbling on weak legs, but not out there with them. I glanced back as Liberty pulled the door closed behind us.

Then I almost tripped over the exposed railway tracks.

The mining cart had crashed into a case across the room, leaving shattered glass around it.

Someone grabbed my arm to steady me. I looked around.

"Haven? And Elena? What are you doing here?" I asked.

Elena clasped her hands together. "Helping! We were watching you on the cameras and hoping the state police would arrive in time to help Dennis since we're not sure who else we can trust but it was getting too dangerous for you."

"I . . . What?" I couldn't make sense of her words. And I desperately needed to sit down or fall down. I staggered to the safe and collapsed on that.

The door handle rattled. I flinched.

"Let's move away from the door in case they decide to start firing through it," Liberty said calmly. She hauled me up again as she strode past.

Haven took my other arm, and between them they hustled me down the room, with Elena bouncing ahead and glancing back to check our progress. I might have heard sirens in the distance, or maybe the wailing was in my ears.

"I think I'm missing some important pieces of information," I mumbled, mostly to myself.

Liberty's gaze cut toward me, a spark of laughter in her eyes. "We'll explain everything, once you're safe."

# Chapter Twenty-Four

SO, YEAH, THAT was exciting.

But the dramatic part is over, and sorting out the details took much, *much* longer, so I'll summarize. It turned out Jerk was a member of the police force, so I guess the police-sheriff rivalry only affected the honest employees. The state police took over, and maybe some federal agents. I'm not really sure, but I answered a lot of questions. I lied as little as I could, which still meant a fair number of lies, but what's the point of telling the truth when people won't believe you? I made it sound like I found clues Reggie had left behind, and put some things together when Macario showed up, and Victor had given away the rest. If nothing else, I'm sure my explanation was rambling and confused enough that they would never suspect me of being involved in the criminal plot. I'm not sure they suspected me of having all my wits.

I slept most of the next day, and when I finally dragged myself to the museum late in the afternoon, Peyton sent me home again and gave me the rest of the week off.

"Just the week? Or are you trying to fire me?"

"Fire you? Why on earth would I do that? I wish you'd brought your concerns about Reggie to me earlier, but that is a minor complaint. Though I will understand if you don't want to come back, I hope to see you next week, or earlier if you'd like to join Gloria and me for lunch one day. I think we would like to get to know you better."

*Gulp. Deep breath.*

"I think I would like that too. And I'll definitely be back next week."

I went home and started unloading the shipping container so I could sleep in my own bed. I'd only moved three boxes into the house before people started showing up to help. I recognized barely a third of them. Elena said Dennis was busy at the sheriff's office, where things were still in an uproar, but she had recruited some muscular cousins who had the furniture where I wanted it within half an hour. Elena distracted the cats while Anne Marie replaced my locks. (Elena couldn't have cats at home because two of her kids were allergic, and she'd already called dibs on cat sitting if I ever left town overnight.)

One of Wilma's exes (pretty sure there was a good story there and I looked forward to hearing it one day) showed up with a charcoal barbecue and a cooler full of meat. Buns, side dishes, drinks, ice, and desserts showed up as if by magic, so we had food for everyone by the time the pod was empty.

Then I had the second party at my house in a week. Also the second party I'd thrown in my adult life. I still had nowhere near enough furniture to seat everyone, but somehow chairs and folding tables appeared from Shelley's house and shed and out of the back of trucks. It was a nice evening, so we sat outside, which made me feel a little better about all the strangers around. I'd met so many new people I wouldn't remember any of their names. Elena had strongly discouraged anyone from asking me to recount what had happened, which I appreciated, even if I suspected it was in part because she enjoyed telling her version of it so much.

As dusk fell, we watched the bats fly overhead, catching bugs. Liberty lounged back in her chair, drinking from a longneck bottle.

I sat next to her. "Have I thanked you yet? It's been a little hectic lately, so I might have forgotten."

Her shoulders shook with a silent laugh. "You could say that. I've never seen so many confused law enforcement agents."

"I'm confused, and I know a lot more than they do. It's a good thing you and Macario didn't say anything on record that would contradict what we had to say later."

Macario had an optimistic belief in the American regard for civil liberties and had refused to discuss anything that didn't directly relate to his identity. When Liberty showed up, Victor told Elena to keep her in the front room until further notice. He'd left Macario in an office under the watchful eye of an innocent deputy and headed to the museum to collect me. Elena told Liberty about Victor's order, of course. (Sheesh, Victor, it's like you have no concept of female friendship.) Liberty and Elena figured out that Victor had slipped out the back way, found that suspicious, and guessed he might assume I'd be easier to intimidate than Liberty or Macario. They called Dennis and rushed to the museum to rescue me.

I still get a little choked up thinking about it.

"We got lucky." Liberty smiled. "The whole town is in an uproar, which of course people love. Half are now claiming they knew all along those two were bad news, even though Victor won the race for sheriff by a landslide, and Dave Rochambeau was pretty popular too."

"Who? Oh, you mean Jerk. I know him well enough to call him by his nickname."

She chuckled. "Hey, did Elena tell you? Reggie was actually listed in the police files as a source or something."

"Yeah. I was wrong about the blackmail."

It now sounded like Victor and Jerk had targeted Reggie because he was such a loner he'd make a good fall guy if things went wrong. They'd recruited him for mysterious *undercover work*. He was only supposed to open the back door when needed and make sure nobody else touched the bags of money and drugs. But he hadn't been quite the dummy they assumed. He had figured out what was really happening and saw a chance to escape his mediocre life. Of course, now Victor was trying to throw all the blame on Reggie and Fausto as conveniently dead scapegoats, but he and Jerk hadn't gotten their stories straight before they were arrested, and Jerk was trying to blame Victor. Macario had narrowly avoided being scooped up as someone who *must be* one of the criminals, but fortunately his newspaper rallied a few Mexican leaders to intervene on his behalf, while Liberty and I did our best to clear his name from here.

I sipped the cocktail Jenny had thrust into my hand. I had no idea what was in it and suspected it packed a bigger punch than the fruity flavor suggested. "I guess the police just have to hire a new employee to replace Jerk, but how will they handle the sheriff's position?"

"Dennis and the other senior deputy will share responsibilities until they can have a special election. Elena says Dennis will run, but I'm not sure Dennis knows that yet. It could be tricky, since anyone currently in law enforcement will have to convince the public that they weren't part of the drug ring."

"I guess that's good. For me, I mean." I glanced around. No one seemed to be listening to us, and our voices wouldn't carry far amidst the babble of other conversations. "If everyone is busy throwing the blame on Victor and Jerk, maybe they won't have time to see the holes in our story about finding Fausto's body."

"Mm. Good thing they have that drug money and two suspects in custody. Pretty sure they're going to ignore everything they don't understand and call it a win."

"I'm alive, so it feels like a win to me."

"We're all glad of that. You'd be hard to replace."

I had a long list of things to be grateful for. Being alive was first, but I also had a home, a job I could like, new friends, and a community. I might not know the community well, but they hadn't shunned me despite my dramatic entrance to their town, which I took as a good sign. And while most of my new friends didn't yet know much about me, I thought I might, one day, trust some of them enough to share. For now, it was odd but nice to have Liberty know the truth and still accept me. And Macario, who would head back to Mexico soon but wanted to keep in touch.

Toby padded over and put his huge head in my lap. I rubbed his ears and ignored the drool on my shorts. A child ran by with a frozen fruit pop, her lips and chin dyed blue. A little later I'd browse the dessert offerings. I might even try talking to some strangers, or at least the people I knew. For the moment, I was content to relax and watch the sky fade to indigo.

I tried to identify what I was feeling and finally came up with the word *content.* Strange that the crazy week would leave me feeling that way. Maybe because I'd been anxious about all the things that could go wrong, and now that so much had gone wrong, I could relax. I'd gotten the bad stuff out of the way, so it should be clear sailing from here. After all, I wasn't likely to stumble on criminal activity again in this small town.

Right?

## The End

## Acknowledgments

Thank you to Phil Miller and Kate Wavrik for suggestions and checking details on the geology, and to Natalie Reid for sharing her psychic experiences to help me with Petra's.

# More Books by Kris Bock

## The Accidental Detective series

Book 1: *Something Shady at Sunshine Haven*

Book 2: *Something Deadly on Desert Drive*

Book 3: *Someone Cruel in Coyote Creek*

Book 4: *Someone Missing from Malapais Mountain*

Book 5: *Someone Murderous at The Midnight Motel*

Book 6: *Someone Rotten Riding the Rails*

## The Accidental Billionaire Cowboys series

Book 1: *The Billionaire Cowboy's Christmas*

Book 2: *Charming the Billionaire Cowboy*

Book 3: *The Billionaire Cowboy's Proposition*

Book 4: *A Baby for the Billionaire Cowboy*

Book 5: *The Billionaire Cowgirl's Christmas*

*Available now at your favorite online retailer!*

## About the Author

Kris Bock writes romance, mystery, and suspense. Learn more about Kris and her books at the Kris Bock website. Get a free cat café novella, mystery stories, recipes, and more when you sign up for the Kris Bock newsletter.

In Kris's mystery series, the Accidental Detective, a witty journalist solves mysteries in Arizona and tackles the challenges of turning fifty. This humorous series starts with Something Shady at Sunshine Haven. Her romantic suspense novels include stories of treasure hunting, archaeology, and intrigue. Readers have called these novels "Smart romance with an Indiana Jones feel."

As for romance, in the Accidental Billionaire Cowboys series, a Texas ranching family wins a fortune in the lottery, which causes as many problems as it solves. Kris's Furrever Friends

Sweet Romance series features the employees and customers at a cat café falling in love with each other and shelter cats. Kris also writes a series with her brother, scriptwriter Douglas J Eboch, who wrote the original screenplay for the movie Sweet Home Alabama. The Felony Melanie series follows the crazy antics of Melanie, Jake, and their friends a decade before the events of the movie.

Thank you for reading

## A Stone Cold Murder

If you enjoyed this book, you can find more from all our great authors at TulePublishing.com, or from your favorite online retailer.

Made in the USA
Las Vegas, NV
25 September 2025